SPIRITUAL WICKEDNESS
IN
HIGH PLACES

STEPH BYERS

Copyright © 2020 Steph Byers

All rights reserved. No part of this publication may be reproduced, distributed, or transmitted in any form or by any means, including photocopying, recording, or other electronic or mechanical methods, without the prior written permission of the publisher, except in the case of brief quotations embodied in critical reviews and certain other noncommercial uses permitted by copyright law.

Any references to historical events, real people, or real places are used fictitiously. Names, characters, and places are products of the author's imagination.

Book cover design Navi' Robins for NorthShore Graphic Studios

www.nsgraphicstudio.com

Interior design by Navi' Robins for NorthShore Graphic Studios

For we wrestle not against flesh and blood, but against principalities, against powers, against the rulers of the darkness of this world, against spiritual wickedness in high PLACES. - Ephesians 6:12

Dedication

This book has been a labor of love. It was at the top of my bucket list, so it was a relief and sense of accomplishment to be able to check it off the list. As a new author, I have learned how important it is to have the support of friends and family as well as those I met throughout this journey. I want to give a special thank you to my son Daniel for his patience, encouragement and guidance. I want to thank all six of my sons for believing that their mom can do anything. My love for my family is beyond measure and I hope this book makes them proud. A special thank you to my mom and dad who received less phone calls from me for the past two years as I worked on this. Finally, I want to dedicate this book to my late husband, Stanley, my beta reader. Through it all, he encouraged me and marveled at my commitment.

Unfortunately, he was unable to read the final copy, but I know he is cheering me on. We shared a deep and abiding love which was truly a gift from God. I'm grateful that Stan was the vessel he used to deliver that gift to me.

TABLE OF CONTENTS

Her Rhythm 1
The Church 7
The Call 15
Lost Innocence 25
Downward Spiral 33
Submit And Obey 46
Betrayed 60
Missing 71
Jen 76
Forsaken 80
New York City 86
Trina 93
The Strip 100
Hope 102
Bent But Not Broken 109
Martha 111
The Return 120
Intuition 123
JJ 126
Revival 129
Epilogue 137

Her Rhythm

Sara slowly opened her eyes, raised her arms to the ceiling, arched her back and stretched across her king-sized bed. The passage of time still wasn't enough to calm the uneasiness she felt upon waking each day. She instinctively felt on guard and fearful until she realized that she was safe and in her own space. Sleep did not bring peace or relief from painful memories.

Reaching for her cell phone on the bedside table she let out an exasperated sigh, "Ugh. 7am, really?" Once again, she had awakened before the soothing music of her alarm filled the room, welcoming her to yet a new day. It was Sunday morning and she had been determined to sleep in. Looking around her spacious apartment she mentally checked off a task on her to do list.

Finding a place to live had been easier than she thought. Within the span of a few weeks of living there, she had fallen in love with the place. The apartment was on the second level of a converted warehouse in the old factory district of the city. The area had charming narrow brick streets. The bricks were old and broken in spots from centuries of hosting foot traffic, horse and buggies and model T cars. Now lined by converted factory buildings they provided passage to skateboards, scooters, and SUVs as the community desperately fought to hold onto the nostalgia of the past.

Sara's building was close to the river just off of West Franklin Street, one of five that made up the district. One of the best things about Elkhart, Indiana was its rivers, at least the way she remembered them. The Elkhart and St. Joseph rivers used to be a pristine body of water, full of fish and soothing sounds. Benches lined its banks and dotted along the sandy places of the shore were large boulders placed by mother nature as a personal invitation to sit a spell. Flowing through the city's largest park, it played host to family reunions, weddings, proposals, and a few baptisms. Parents kept a watchful eye on the little ones who were always drawn to the water. It was a cocoon of good food, wonderful music, giggles and hugs, games, drunk uncles, bossy aunts, and lots and lots of storytelling. It had also become the place for reflection and contemplation during periods of unsteady change in her young life. The river was where she expressed her first crush to an older boy who told her that she was too little. It was the place that received her tears when she learned of her parents' divorce and it was where she visited to gather enough courage to confront life challenges. The memories of it had helped to bring some relief throughout her troubled times. To her disappointment, the poison that found its way into her life was now reflected in her beloved river that had been saturated with pollution and neglect.

Being home brought back many fond memories of Sara's grandparents. She could hear her grandfather heading off to work at the foundry. In every season, he left before sunrise dressed in his white shirt and freshly pressed khakis, grabbed his black lunch pail, kissed her grandmother goodbye, and headed to work in that hell hole. Her grandmother made sure that his lunch pail was full of good food and hot coffee. It held two large sandwiches, two pieces of fruit, whatever vegetable was left over from dinner the night before, a thick slice of chocolate or coconut cake, all homemade of course, and a large thermos of hot coffee. Sara always wondered why he needed so much food because she could barely pick it up. It left the house full every morning and returned empty every evening. She later learned that he shared his lunch with others. He returned each night with the thickest black soot all over him. Happy to be home and his eyes full of laughter and kindness.

Shaking the memories from her mind, Sara eased out of bed. Like so many other things, nothing was quite the same and never would be again. She had to remain committed to the task at hand, her purpose for returning.

After brewing a pot of coffee, she sat on the black leather barstool at the kitchen counter and skimmed through the local paper. Slowly rotating her head, she took in her surroundings and allowed herself to be in the moment. She realized that the kitchen was her warm and comfy place. It had thick lacquered shelves that revealed the natural grain of the oak wood anchored to a red brick wall, floating between richly stained mahogany cabinets. The gold countertop with flecks of silver and black rested on the center island. The kitchen was equipped with stainless-steel Viking appliances meant for a master chef to enjoy. The flooring revealed extra wide distressed cherry planks covered haphazardly with deep cream shaggy throw rugs.

"My kitchen hugs me whenever I enter," she thought. Holding a large cup of coffee with both hands and slowly sipping the warm caramel colored liquid, Sara began planning her day.

The move back to Elkhart just two weeks earlier was uneventful. Using an agency to locate, secure and furnish the apartment allowed her to maintain her privacy. The kitchen had been fully stocked with food by the agency, including her favorite wine. As planned, she would not have to go out into the town for weeks. This would give her time to think, figure out a routine and establish her rhythm. The town was so small that it only took one person to notice her and everyone would know that she had returned. She had only told one person from her new life that she was going home. It was the only person she had learned to trust.

Elkhart, "The City with a Heart," is the city's motto. To the unknowing it is easy to assume that this was a nice welcoming place where everyone got along. Many outsiders misunderstood the city's motto. It is not a human heart but an Elk's heart. Incongruously, hunting Elk was allowed. The city was founded in 1832 and the name was actually derived from the Potawatomi Indians who called the small island that rested where the Elkhart and St. Joe rivers converge forming an Elk's heart because of its shape. The city name and motto are a symbol and recognition of the place where the two rivers join. Brotherly love may not have been free flowing throughout the city, but neighborly love was abundant. It was a welcoming little town as long as people remained in their areas of the city. The railroad provided a natural segregation line. Whites lived north of the tracks and Blacks south. The Italians stayed to the northwest parts of the city and the far east flowed into Mennonite and Amish country.

During the Jim Crow era and segregation , Blacks only went north of the tracks to work in the band instrument factories, foundry or to clean houses for rich white folk. The Black community was a large neighborhood. Families lived within a few blocks or streets of each other. The streets throughout the neighborhood were lined with trees on each side, the branches that reached across to intertwine, creating a natural arch. People knew each other and maintained a sense of responsibility for the other. Everything you needed could be found within the neighborhood. The Cozy Corner Tavern provided a stiff drink, funky music and good ole home cooking. There were six buildings, all contained within two blocks, where you could find a good meal or somebody to keep you warm at night. The pool hall maintained a cast of shady characters. Little boys ran around the buildings laughing and playing, but little girls were not allowed in the area. The community grocery store at Indiana Avenue and 6th Street and the gas station on the corner of Indiana and Benham Ave, just south of the tracks, were Black owned. It may not have been a perfect place; however, it was filled with pride and a sense of community.

As with most small towns, privacy didn't exist. If you had business, everyone had their nose in it. Life was easy but could get complicated. Unless somebody new moved in, relationships were easily recycled. Kids playing with friends unknowingly played with a half sibling. Grandparents raise the children of their teenage kids as their own and often one would find out that their aunt and uncle were really their cousin. The neighborhoods lived by a natural beat, their own rules of right and wrong, while coping with the interchanging life and duality of living in barely connected worlds, the one north of the tracks to work and south of the tracks to live and thrive.

Now, post integration and the time of Black Presidents, Sara's siblings, parents, and relatives were all still living in Elkhart and active in every aspect of running the city. Things had changed, the city was embracing modernization and was committed to holding onto historical architecture and some cultural norms. She was proud to see that her family was a part of it all. In an odd way she felt grateful to see that they had moved on with their lives and were all doing well.

Just shy of her eighteenth birthday, she had disappeared. No one had seen her, and all leads to what happened had dried up. Eventually, the police stopped working on the case. Many thought she had run away, and for a short period, the rumors had morphed into stories of abduction, mental illness and murder, as speculation feed by the unknow tried to fill the gaps and provide answers in response to

SPIRITUAL WICKEDNESS IN HIGH PLACES

people's need to know. The truth was much more intriguing and nefarious. One late summer night she walked out of her mother's house into the backyard and into the wilderness. In the end, her experiences had helped to build her confidence and taught her how to survive. She learned what true evil looked like. But most of all, she now had a clear understanding that in some situations no one wins.

What she needed to do would horrify some, sicken others, and bring a sense of satisfaction and maybe pride to a few. It was time to focus her mind and energy to the task at hand, getting ready for church. Attending church was a distant memory and a place that she promised herself long ago that she would never set foot in again. The time had come to break that promise.

The Church

Sara looked into the mirror and smiled. Feeling confident that she had nailed the small-town church girl look she turned from side to side admiring the simple white sun dress with a subtle flowery print and a light blue mid-length sweater that hid the tattoo on her shoulder. A friend had helped her hide a scar by having a lily tattooed over it. The lily was called the Rose of Sharon. It was the symbol of purity, inner perfection, and beauty. Her makeup was minimal, a little color on her cheeks, a raspberry tint lipstick and just enough mascara to slightly lengthen her eyelashes. She topped the look off with a navy sun hat and a small navy purse. She wore a single cross necklace and had decided to wear her hair in a simple braid that draped the side of her left shoulder, stopping just shy of her waist. Not bad, she thought.

Dressing up like this was foreign to her now. It was a costume that many people put on every Sunday to play a role that masked who they really were. She had come to learn that the fanciest dresser, the loudest voices, and the most flamboyant worshipers were people usually filled with evil thoughts and deeds. They were enabled by those who helped them live the lie including preachers who coddled them by refusing to teach the truth. She took one last look, winked, tilted her hat slightly to the right, slipped her sunglasses on, and picked up her phone to call a taxi. The dispatcher indicated that the driver was only two minutes away. Small town living at its best.

SPIRITUAL WICKEDNESS IN HIGH PLACES

A black Nissan Altima pulled up in front of Sara's building. A taxi sign was prominently displayed in the lower right-hand corner of the windshield. The driver's picture and identification were taped to the back right side window, indicated that the driver was Jason Edward James. He had a five-star rating, which was rare because there is always one idiot that believes no one is perfect, regardless of how great the service. Sara opened the door and eased into the back seat. She took off her hat and sunglasses, just as Jason greeted her with a "Blessed Sunday, Miss Bouche." He pronounced her name Booch. She looked up correcting him, "My name is pronounced Bow-Shay." As their eyes locked a glimmer of familiarity quickly evolved into full recognition.

"Sara?! Oh my God! Sara Robinson?!" Jason called out her name in shock and disbelief. "Is that you, when did you get back? I thought you were dead. We all thought that you were dead!" he rambled, the rapid fire of questions and declarations revealed his surprise and struggle with disbelief. As quickly as he started, he abruptly stopped, starring at her, awaiting answers. She sat silent trying to decide how to handle...Jason? He was 22 years old when she left, four years ahead of her in school. She remembered that he walked with a slight limp and seemed a little strange. Sara always considered him smart but lazy and kept her distance from him. She could not figure out why some of the prettiest older girls in school liked him so much. In a strange way she felt sorry for him. Now, he was driving a taxi. There had been rumors around town that his alcoholic father had beat his mother while she was pregnant with him. The trauma, caused by the beating, sent her into labor and Jason was born six weeks premature. No one thought he would live. Now she saw a well-groomed older man, who seemed a little shy. His car was clean and fresh. He had water and magazines in the back seat for his riders. He obviously took the taxi job seriously. Here she sat, staring into a pair of big brown eyes and a white toothy grin, patiently waiting for a response.

"Jason, my goodness, you're so handsome. Time has been good to you," she deflected. "How are you?"

"Oh, I have no complaints. I do my best," looking away as if to keep her from seeing the truth in his eyes. "I see that you are going over to the church this morning. It's only five minutes away and I will have you there in a blink of an eye."

Sara found herself looking at the back of his head and searching for a decision on how to handle him. "Jason, how do you like driving a taxi?" she asked.

"It's ok. I do it weekends. I stay to myself; this little town is too nosey. I try to keep my ear to the ground and live a humble life," he said looking at her through the rearview mirror.

Sara's heart ached as she listened to him. "Listen Jason, I will need a driver while I am here. How about you drive me around when you're not working, and I'll pay you. How does that sound?" she asked.

His eyes lit up and his grin spread from ear to ear. "Really? Why yes, of course, anything you want Sara," he said as he pulled in front of the church.

Reaching over the front seat she slid a hundred-dollar bill into his hand. "Oh, and Jason, I'm going to need you to be quiet about seeing me. My privacy is important. You say nothing to no one. Understand? Because if you do, well… let's not think about consequences right now. After all its Sunday," she said staring directly into his eyes and not blinking.

"I understand," he replied as he turned away from her. Looking into the rearview mirror he slightly lowered his eyelids. Instinctually he wanted to remind her that he was a man. He hated the thought of being seen as weak. However, he could not help but consider the potential consequences of sharing her secret and decided that it might be in both of their best interests if he stayed silent. He made a mental note that she had not answered his questions.

"Now pick me up in 40 minutes. I want you sitting outside waiting for me," she directed him as she stepped out of the car, put on her hat and sunglasses and headed for the entrance of the church.

Jason watched Sara walk into the church. He smiled thinking that she had grown into a beautiful hot piece of ass. Feeling a sense of uneasiness, he drove off trying to figure out why she was so adamant about not letting anyone know she was back in town and what that meant for him. In the meantime, he would take her up on making some extra money.

Stepping into the church lobby was like walking back into time. There were three sets of oversized double doors leading into the sanctuary. Blonde wood floors adorned with deep red-carpet runners. Benches and huge floral arrangements were placed between each set. The stained glass in each door was beautiful and prevented anyone from looking into the sanctuary or out of it. The doors left and right of the center had images of lilies and lambs. The center entrance displayed the crucifixion of Christ. Six male ushers stood stately waiting to grant entrance to all worshipers. Each one dressed in the traditional black church uniform, black suits, white shirts, red ties, and white gloves. Sara always wondered why they wore gloves. The men sized her up right away, all hoping that she would walk through their doors so they could get a good look. Dirty old men, she thought.

Usher Johnson approached her, holding out a program. He smiled, just shy of literally drooling, and said, "Welcome to the Church, young lady." His chest was puffed up with pride because he was a Deacon and the head usher responsible for the center doors. That, at least in his mind, gave him status. He had been opening those same doors for thirty years. Sara did not respond to him, intentionally snubbing him by deliberately depriving him of her attention she walked past him to the doors left of center. Nodding at the usher, she took a program, and walked into the sanctuary. Here we go, she thought.

As she entered the doors, the choir director signaled the choir to stand. They were dressed in black robes adorned with a shiny bright red satin stripe down each sleeve, a red scarf, draped around their necks that stopped just below their hands. Each end of the scarf were gold crosses. As the organist played a few chords, the director motioned for the choir to stand and start swaying back and forth. It seemed like minutes; yet it was only a few seconds that they swayed in silence. With a slight nod and tilt of his right had the Director signaled for the choir to begin. The bass section forcefully sang out "My God!" followed by the soprano section, then the tenor, and lastly the alto section. Each singing "My God!" and holding the notes in perfect harmony. It was as if they were braided together and it brought everyone to their feet. They continued singing "My God is an Awesome God; He reigns from Heaven Above." Sara had heard that song a million times but the way the Black Church does it always shook her to the core with the powerful statement of fact. As the choir held the attention of the members, Sara eased into the last seat in the third row from the back. The exact same spot she occupied years ago. This seat would allow her to easily leave and it provided a vantage point to see everyone and more importantly, watch to see who was looking at her. Veiled by her sunglasses and hat she quietly watched.

The sanctuary was beautiful. There were four bays of seating. Each isle leading to the pulpit. The balcony was six rows deep. The pulpit was built high above the main floor seating. It was the highest place in the sanctuary. Six steps surrounded the stage. The choir was seated directly behind the pulpit. From the main floor you had to look up to see the Pastor as he preached the word. Only ordained pastors were allowed to stand in that sacred space. Everyone else spoke from a podium on the main floor. A large crucifix hung high on the wall and was long enough that those walking by could touch the feet of Christ.

When the music stopped, she noticed those who turned and glanced at her as the pastor asked everyone to be seated. Several women did a double take. The lack of gasps and finger pointing was a good indication that no one recognized her, but she noticed their curiosity growing as they leaned over to whisper in the ear of those next to them. She watched the grapevine at work and counted three beats: one, two, three then turn and look back, each person following the same rhythm, hoping to turn in the right direction and catch a glimpse of the newcomer.

And there he was. "Church!" he bellowed. "Can I have your attention, Church?" Pastor Christopher Stanfield. He was a powerful man. Tall, lean, and handsome. His hair was naturally wavy, and she noticed that his temples had grayed, giving him a distinguished look. Seeing him, her spiritual father again made her nervous. The pastor enjoyed a reputation of being a very charismatic yet soft-spoken and gentle man, dedicated to his wife and the Church. Her gazed fixated on the pastor. She watched him nod and shout "Amen!" to someone sitting on the first pew. His wife, Rose, stood as he stretched out his hand towards her. Stepping from behind the dais, he walked over to meet his wife as she approached the three steps leading up to the pulpit. She gracefully ascended and took his hand. Pastor Stanfield leaned over and kissed her cheek, then escorted her to the first lady's chair on the right side of his throne.

Time had been kind to her as well. Rose was a pleasant looking lady, quiet and reserved. It was said that before she found God, or he found her, she was a loose and fast woman. The men liked her, and she liked the men. As a couple, they were known to party hard and fight even harder. No one knew their salvation story but their commitment to the church could not be denied. Now, as a loving and faithful couple, they openly displayed their affection for each other. However, their demeanor did not stop the ladies from flirting with him, each one vying to replace the pastor's wife one day.

As Pastor Christopher Stanfield launched into his sermon, Sara looked around to see if there were other familiar faces. Some things never change; sitting in the second pew behind the deacons as he did years ago was Associate Pastor Calvin Peterson. He had aged, too. His square jaw, long grey sideburns, thick neck, and bugged eyes were all older and bigger than she had remembered. He stood the entire time the choir was singing, looking around and clapping. Making sure that he was seen by all. Calvin was a bachelor. As a young man, he had not been handsome, but he was charming. He dressed to impress and wore an intoxicating cologne. He was what the old folks called a "Cat Daddy," meaning a lady's man. He never married and when asked why not, he would effortlessly state, "The Lord's work takes up all of my time and the Church is my wife. And she is a jealous wife at that!" You would think this would stop his pursuers. But if you believe that, you have never been to church. To the contrary, she had often seen women in the church vying for his attention. Now seeing the two men flaunting and acting so pious made her more determined to do what she needed to do.

Pastor Stanfield began wrapping up his sermon shouting about the goodness of God. The members responded, yelling Amen and hallelujah, as they waved hands and white hankies at him. The organist accompanied the Pastor's words. As he raised his voice, the music became more frenzied, and as he lowered it, the music slowed. As if on cue the Missionary Board members, the baby saints, and the self-righteous started cheering the Pastor on and breaking into their holy dance. The Missionaries did it out of obligation. The baby saints were feeling something, not clearly understanding what and jerked awkwardly back and forth. They normally ended up on the floor, rolling around or falling back onto the pew as if they would faint. Ushers rushed to be by their side, fanning their faces or covering up their unfortunately exposed body parts. The self-righteous danced without breaking a sweat or missing a beat, while holding onto their hats, wigs, or ties. Glistening from sweat, slobber and tears they exhausted themselves and one by one returned to their seats.

    Sara stood and eased out of the door unnoticed, or so she thought. Pastor Stanfield watched as the mysterious woman left and wondered who she was and what she wanted. On her way-out Sara picked up a flyer, quickly exited the building and slipped into the back seat of the Altima. "Perfect timing Jason take me back to my place and let me out in the back please," she said.

The Call

Sara was thirteen when she found God. She often recalled the day it happened. Her mother had sent her to pick up a loaf of bread, two dozen eggs, a pound of ground beef and an eight pack of Pepsi from Wilts corner market. Not wanting to respond, she ignored her mom calling out to her from the bottom of the stairs. The demand to go to the store invaded her imagination and disrupted the journey she was on within her book. She could hear the frustration in her mother's voice, a sign that she was annoyed by the lack of an immediate response. This was not new; Sara loved books. It was a way to escape her bedroom and travel all around the world. Books opened up and accepted her into new dimensions, shutting out her reality. Imagining smells, hearing sounds, and eavesdropping into the lives of fictional characters provided relief of daily responsibilities and gave her an opportunity to be selfish.

"Sara, Sara Jean! Get your lazy behind down here, girl!" her mother yelled. Jarred back to the confines of four walls, she yelled "Yes, ugh, I'm comin'!"

As she reached the top of the staircase, her mother began scolding her. "Girl, you deaf! And I heard you, young lady, don't you yes me! What do you say, yes what?" She threatened.

Sara hesitated; she knew how to respond but it always stuck in her throat. Her mother wanted the show of respect whether one meant it or not, however her father detested the use of ma'am or sir. He always told her that most people who demand it don't deserve it. But she was not stupid, to not say it would result in being slapped so hard that her teeth would rattle or worse, being grabbed by the forearm and jerked around. Her mother meant business all the time and had zero tolerance for sass. Sara looked at her feet and quietly responded, "Yes ma'am," forcing the words to come out while simultaneously to keep her anger from showing in her tone.

Her mother gave her the grocery list and told her to hurry up. "Don't mess around either, you got twenty minutes, there and back, now get on, girl!" she yelled.

Taking the list, making sure not to snatch it , she brushed past her mother and quickly headed towards the door. Sara stepped outside and noticed how good the sun felt on her skin. It was a warm autumn day and her favorite time of the year. The walk to the store led her past the abandoned school and the older boys playing basketball. The net was missing from the rim, along with the swish sound that came with the direct hit of the ball. On auto pilot, she mindlessly plodded out the one block east and five blocks north to the store. The leaves caught her attention. They were changing color, and as the wind gently blew, they chased each other, swirling and rustling as if they were choreographed. The air smelled fresh and clean and the slight chill reminded her that snow would be on the ground soon. About halfway to her destination she approached the little white church. As was usual there were cars parked at the church. Regardless of the day of the week, people were present, and some activity was underway. Sara could hear the organ playing a block away and the closer she got to the church she could hear a woman singing.

The voice was beautiful, unlike anything she had ever heard and unique, in a special way, the tone was fluid and easy. The words to the song captured her. "Take me back, take me back dear Lord, to the place where I first received you. Take me back, take me back dear Lord, where I first believed."

The words grabbed her and pulled her inside as if she were tethered to an invisible cord, unable to resist or turn away. She walked up the steps, entered the door propped open by a brick and sat in the back, mesmerized. The woman singing was a girl her age! Her voice was strong, rich, and effortless. The song wrapped around her heart and a tear trickled down her cheek. The words touched a place deep in her soul that hinted at something familiar, like a time, experience or feeling just beyond her ability to recall. Sara knew about God, and on and off had attended church on Easter and Christmas, but it did not mean anything to her. Attending was something she was made to do along with her siblings. This was different…this feeling was causing something to awaken inside of her. She could feel the words. It was not a song that she was hearing but a calling.

As she listened, tears flowing she caught the attention of the organist. His name was Maurice, but everyone called him Sugar. He saw her when she walked in and was immediately taken in by her simple beauty.

"My, my" he thought, "What a precious little dove, so simple, so beautiful, so elegant."

Personally, she was not his type. too young for one, and too female for the other. But he could not help thinking that she was special. He noticed her wiping her eyes and nodded to a woman sitting on the first pew. Turning in the direction of Sugar's nod, the woman spotted Sara and immediately got up and approached her. "Hello, sweetheart. Can I sit with you for a while?" she asked. Sara nodded yes and the woman eased into the pew and sat beside her.

"I'm Rose, but in the church, they call me Lady Rose. What's your name?" she asked.

"Sara."

SPIRITUAL WICKEDNESS IN HIGH PLACES

"What a beautiful name. Did you know that an especially important woman in the Bible was named Sara?" she asked.

"Sort of," Sara replied looking down.

Lady Rose continued to chatter along. Like background noise during a good movie, she tried to tune her out, growing more annoyed by the minute. She stated that this was choir rehearsal for the young people in the church. Sara remained mesmerized by the music and was startled when Lady Rose, with one fluid move, gently placed a right arm around her shoulders and a left had on Sara's knee. Turning to look directly at her, she asked, " Honey do you believe in God and have you accepted Jesus Christ as her Lord and Savior?" Sara hesitated before responding. She felt anger and frustration invading her sense of peace and her desire to enjoy the music.

Moving her shoulders back and forth, trying to wiggle away without being rude, she heard a voice. At first, she thought someone behind her was whispering into her ear. She turned and look at the empty seat behind her expecting to see someone sitting there. Facing forward, the voice spoke again.

"She will guide you, follow her," it said.

Not knowing if the voice was her own thoughts or something else, Sara looked down, suddenly feeling weak and helpless, unable to utter a word. Rose tightened her arm and pulled her close. What initially seemed like an intrusion now felt like comfort and safety.

"Sara, do you want to accept Jesus as your Lord and Savior?" She asked

Sara nodded. Holding hands, they stood and walked down the aisle to the front of the church. The choir stopped singing and turned their attention to the two standing before them. They understood what was going on and could barely hold their excitement as Lady Rose announced that God had called out to one of his sheep. They erupted in applause and cheers, celebrating the blessing of conversion. Abruptly, Lady Rose raised her hand, and on cue the sanctuary fell silent, except for occasional whispers of "Amen" and "Thank you, Jesus" as she led Sara through the prayer of Salvation. Sara felt warm inside, and within a blink of an eye, something within her changed. A spiritual door had opened and stepping through it she felt like a cloudiness had been removed, and a family long forgotten was somehow now familiar.

She was changed; she was home.

Choir members hugged and welcomed her. One of them asked Sara what had brought her to the Church. Not sure how long she had been there, she remembered her assigned task; the store, twenty minutes there and back. Her mother was going to kill her. She had been gone for two hours. As she was rushing toward the doors Lady Rose called out to her to come back on Saturday for youth services. Sara agreed to do so and ran the rest of the way to the store.

Mr. Wilts stood in front of his store as he had done at the same time every day for the past twenty years. Each day prior to closing, he would step outside and look up and down the block. It was part of his routine. Her mom told her that he was just being nosey. But her grandmother told her that there was a time when Whites rode through the community harassing Black people. The later in the day it got, danger increased. Mr. Wilts would stand watch to make sure the people running late got in and out of his store without being harmed. Although times had changed, it was an old habit that he refused to let go. He noticed Sara running towards him and opened the door while motioning her to hurry. He told her that she had ten minutes because he was ready to go home. Everyone in the neighborhood knew Jen and her children. All of them were good kids and Sara, being the oldest was admired for being so responsible at such a young age. Although he was eager to call it a night and go home, he could not turn her away. She quickly grabbed the items on her mother's list, thanked Mr. Wilts and ran all the way home.

Entering the house, Sara was still feeling a buzz from her time at the church. She was floating on a cloud, her feet hovering a few inches above the ground. Having found a new home, she felt invigorated as she walked into the front hall. With bags of groceries in each arm, she hesitated in the entryway before entering the kitchen and stood still for a moment, closing her eyes to bask in the gentle light of the setting sun streaming through the door. She felt the warmth of God's love pouring through the door of salvation that had just opened for her. Like a helium filled balloon her newfound happiness and its promise rose higher and higher within her. Feeling as if she would float away, she twirled around on her toes, bags in hand as her mother walked in and saw her.

"Girl, where the hell have you been?" her mother asked, her voice rough and accusatory. "You meet up with some boy? I gave you ten minutes, and you left three hours ago!"

Sara bit her tongue instead of telling her mother that it was actually twenty minutes given and two hours gone. She hated that she was being accused of meeting up with a boy. She was a tomboy and thinking of boys in that way was the farthest thing from her mind. What did she care about a boy? All she wanted to do was read books, and the only thing that stopped her from doing that was her mother, not some boy.

"Sara, I asked you a question. Where've you been?"

"I was at church, Ma," Sara answered as if her newfound faith would shield her from her mother's wrath. She continued, cautiously sharing, barely able to contain her excitement. "I was walking to the store, and then I heard the most beautiful voice singing in the church.

So, I went in to listen and see who was singing. I met some of the church people. They were having a choir rehearsal for young people. A woman, Lady Rose, talked to me, and she helped me get saved—"

"Stop lying, Sara Jean! You were out with a boy fooling around!"

The world stopped turning for a moment when Sara felt a hard smack on her cheek from her mother's calloused, worn hand. A stinging pain rippled on Sara's face. Sara had been slapped before, but this one punctured her mood and heart. As was the case with many of her mother's punishments, she hadn't done anything to deserve such swift and harsh abuse. Her mother would slap her for what she was thinking. She could never figure out exactly what it was that she was thinking about that resulted in being punished. She had learned to live with it, and at times could anticipate the swinging palm in enough time to avoid being its intended contact. But this time instead of crying and hating her mother for the rebuke as she usually did, she swallowed and blinked away the tears trying to pool at her cheeks.

"Ma, I was at the church. I promise I wasn't out fooling around with a boy. I was at church with Lady Rose, and I got saved. You can ask her if you'd like, and she'll tell you I was there. It's the truth."

"Ain't no truth to that!" Clenching her teeth, her mother's jaw tightened along with her fist, and her anger continued to mount as Sara refused to admit to something she didn't do. "Little girl, I don't know who you think I'm, but stupid ain't it. You bet not let me find out that you been wit some boy and you best believe that I'm going to find out what is true and don't you ever contradict me again, in this life or the next! Am I understood?"

Losing her internal battle to not cry, the tears changed from a few drops to a constant flow, she bowed her head and moved past her mother to go into the kitchen and begin preparing dinner. "Yes ma'am," came out of a sore throat and wilting voice. She didn't like the

SPIRITUAL WICKEDNESS IN HIGH PLACES

sad feeling that was befalling her at this moment, and she desperately wanted to go back to the church and feel that joy that had so graciously enveloped her.

While preparing dinner Sara reflected on her experience at the church. She liked Lady Rose and loved the music. The choir was very friendly, and everyone started calling her Sister Sara. She liked that Maurice, the choir director, wanted to hear her sing and invited her to choir practice. She smiled at the thought of having a second family, one that believed the words that came out of her mouth and showed love more openly. The people at the church were each different in their own way. But they all worked together in harmony like the dinner she was making. As she browned the ground beef, adding onions, seasoning, bell peppers and mushrooms, then folding in the tomato sauce, she thought of how everything came together for something good, united by the sauce, which is like God, covering everything. The sting from the slap returned her focus back to the task at hand, cooking dinner.

She finished making the meal, but her appetite was spoiled, and she chose to go without dinner for the night. Everyone ate in their own rooms, and the kitchen table stayed empty. Usually, Sara would normally eat at the table, but instead she started cleaning the dishes to avoid her mother having something else to get upset about. The dishwater was too hot, and burned her hands, making them red and sore. She scrubbed hard and as fast as she could, wanting to end the day. When she finished, she disappeared to her room and got into bed fully clothed. Sara didn't want to take them off as she closed her eyes and willed herself to imagine the church again. She wanted to remember what that voice sounded like when she first heard it and Lady Rose's soft hand and Maurice's warmness and how they called her "Sister Sara." She even said it to herself into the darkness. "...Brother Maurice, Lady Rose, Sister Sara..." She wanted to remember all of it and hide it in her heart with her new faith. Sara decided to plant God and her new family so deep in the soil of her heart that no one or thing could ever uproot them. And that she did.

From that beautiful fall day and over the next several years, the church became Sara's life. It took some persuading to get her siblings to tag along. At first, she bribed them with candy and the promise of doing their chores for them or extra visits to the park. After a couple of visits and seeing that there were always cookies or treats readily available, they were anxious to attend. The older kids used the time to hang out with friends from school that attend the church services or were a part of the choir. Her two worlds quickly merged together. Wherever she could lend a hand, be it youth work, cleaning or teaching little kids Bible classes, she was eager to help.

Evidence of Sara's love of reading could be found among the dog eared and highlighted pages of her Bible. On Sunday evenings, she would enter her bedroom, close the door, and begin studying the scriptures. It was different from reading other books. This one had a way of making her feel better. It helped her to try to understand and not judge people.

On many occasions when she was not sure what to do when she heard the voice, now a constant companion, giving her insight and understanding. The first time she heard the voice was the day she walked into the church. It was unsettling and a little scary. Now she welcomed and waited to hear it, wondering if it was the voice of God or angels. Unexpectedly it would come upon her, welling up from her heart and amplified her head. When it spoke, the feeling was a sense of knowing. She could argue with the voice, questioning the message and herself. It would always respond by repeating the original message. She was concerned that if it was the voice of God, why was it not a whisper into her ear, versus a sense of knowing and a sound inside her head?

One day she approached Elder Washburn. He was ninety-one years old and the founder of the Church. He could be found most days in the sanctuary sitting in his wheelchair next to one of the pews with his Bible in his lap. Sometimes he sat for hours staring at the statute of Jesus hanging behind the pulpit. Other times he seemed to be praying or talking to himself. Sara told him about the voice, and he told her it was God.

"But Elder, if it is the voice of God, why do I hear it in my head?" she asked.

He looked at her, his eyes cloudy and weak and responded, "Daughter, God lives within you. You will not hear his voice from the outside, but within. Now what you must do, since you have an ear to hear him, is pray and fast so you can discern his voice from your own. Many people cannot do this. His voice will always lead you to what is right even through all of your trials and hurt. Just trust it because you can diminish his voice if you ignore it or turn away. And if you turn away, you will spend the rest of your night wishing you had not."

Sara knew his advice was true, sensing that he was speaking from experience. She thanked him and kissed his cheek. Walking out of the Church she vowed to fast and pray because she wanted to get closer to God. Watching her leave, old Elder Washburn prayed for her, *"God keep her strong and wrap her mind in your grace. Let her trials and tribulations be an acceptable sacrifice unto you and a witness before your people."* Elder Washburn hoped that through his sincere prayer for her, he would find forgiveness and God's favor for himself. His wife Brenda had died several years earlier, and he knew his time was at hand. He just hoped that heaven would be his last stop.

Lost Innocence

Several years had passed since Sara walked by the church and heard the beautiful voice that pulled her inside. Time had moved by quickly while she had become a valued member of the church community. Lady Rose had grown to love and depended on her. She had become her right hand including helping cook and serve when they had guests over for dinner. Lady Rose had become a second mom to her. She was just gentle and easy. Her laugh was contagious, and she was always laughing. When Sara was with her, it was like she was special, and she was doing God's work. Rose would tell her that sometimes you just had to let things that bother you go and focus on the things that bring you joy. "When we can no longer do that, well, heaven help us!" she would say.

With high school graduation in two weeks, Sara had become the center of attention at church. Home life was different. At home she was responsible for caring for her siblings. At church she shared responsibilities as part of a team. Her mom didn't seem to notice much. She was exhausted, working two jobs and trying to find her way. Sara never hated her mother. She hated having to grow up so fast, not going to prom and just being different than other kids at school.

God had spoken to her heart concerning her mother. One night while reading her Bible, the voice asked her three questions: "What is your mother's favorite color? What did your mother want to be when she grew up? What are your mother's dreams?" it said. At first, Sara shrugged but the voice asked the questions again. Sara did not know the answers to these questions or why she needed to know them. What she knew was the meanness, the absence of love and laughter, the selfishness and the lack of nurturing was missing. That is what she said to the voice.

"Pray for your mother. The enemy comes to kill, to steal and to destroy. If he can kill your dreams, steal your hopes, he will destroy your future. Open your eyes and see the person you call mom and pray for her," said the voice. It was strong yet gentle and Sara pushed it away. After all of her studying and teachings she could not grasped this command from God and for the first time she did what Elder Washington warned her not to do, she ignored the voice of God, opening a small crack, ever so slight in her spiritual foundation. Protecting her siblings was more important to her than trying to understand her mother. She would graduate soon, and she had to prepare for that because God knows her mother would not.

As graduation grew closer everyone began asking her what she was going to do next. This very question opened the door to her anxiety and frustrations. With each passing day, her indecisiveness mounted and the fear of making the wrong decision brought an overwhelming sense of guilt. Several colleges had sent admission letters offering partial scholarships, but she also worried about being able to take care of her siblings and help her mother. They needed her. The battle was between her desire to get away, meet new people and only care for herself versus an overwhelming sense of responsibility to her family. She had learned how to worry; her faith had not taught her how to stop it.

The Church was planning a special event honoring the graduates. Lady Rose asked her to stop by her office around 4:00 p.m. to pick up a special graduation gift. Her excitement made it difficult to focus on anything but the gift, so she decided to go an hour early and pray. She hoped it was a crucifix necklace like the one she noticed around Lady Rose's neck. It was a beautiful rose gold cross accented by red gemstones. The day she noticed and admired it, Lady Rose had just smiled and winked at her.

Sara entered the church and found it dark and quiet. No one seemed to be there. She had noticed Pastor Stanfield's car in the parking lot and figured he had to be somewhere in the building. Walking through the sanctuary, she stopped to pick up Bibles from the pews and place them on the shelf at the back of the church. Several offices were located off a hallway to the right of the Pulpit. Entering the hallway, she noticed that Lady Rose's office was dark, and the door was closed. Glancing further down the hall she sat that the Pastor's door was open, and a soft glowing light emanated from his office. She quietly walked to his door and peeked inside. Pastor Stanfield was sitting at his desk reading his Bible.

"Excuse me Pastor" she said. "Lady Rose asked me to stop by and pick up a gift. I came early to pray. I just wanted you to know that I was here. Do you need anything?", she asked.

"Sara! Praise God. I am so glad that you are here. I want to take a moment to pray with you before the big day in two weeks! Is that okay? Can I pray for you?" he asked. "Lady Rose is running a little late, she'll be here soon, I'm sure of it."

Hesitating, she looked down the hall and back into the office. She noticed the walls were paneled with dark wood and lined with bookshelves. A maroon-colored leather couch with a tufted back was to the left of the doorway. Two paisley covered black and white chairs sat in front of the couch with a round cocktail table between them. She was surprised to see a cabinet with bottles of liquor sitting in back to the right and wondered why it was there. A large stained-glass window facing the parking lot was behind the desk. Light filtering through it cast shadows on the walls. His desk was so large that she doubted he would be able to sit behind it and touch each end at the same time. A picture of Lady Rose and a young girl in an angel winged frame sat on one corner and a marble cross statute sat at the opposite end. Books, paper, and a laptop were spread out in the center.

Pushing back his big leather chair, he stood and smiled at her. He always made her feel nervous. He was powerful. He was God's man. He was her spiritual father. Lady Rose always talked about how much she loved him and how she was thankful that God had placed her by his side to help him. She once told Sara that when God blessed her with a husband one day, she should always remember that trusting and serving him would be her blessing. She said a woman that found a Godly man found a good man.

Sara looked up and said, "Of course, Pastor."

He reached across the desk extending his hands. Sara placed hers into his. They were so big that when he enveloped her hands, she could no longer see them. He started praying for her and rubbing the back of her hands with his thumbs. Gentle relaxing strokes. Other than quick hugs and handshakes during church fellowship, she had never held a man's hands. Her father was not an affectionate man and was very conservative. She had never seen his bare chest and could not remember ever holding onto his hands. But here she was, alone, with the Pastor holding her hands and praying. It felt good. Sara could not remember the prayer; she only remembered his touch. She must have missed the amen because he called her name and asked if she was alright.

"Yes Pastor, I am fine. A little nervous," she said. "Just wanting to get through graduation and decide what I am going to do next."

Pastor Stanfield walked around the desk and closed the door. Pointing towards the door he smiled and told her the Deacons would be there soon to discuss church finances.

"They can wait while you tell me all about your post-graduation plans," he said.

"Pastor, my plans are not clear to me, but I know that everything will be ok. I will let you get back to your work. God will show me the way," she responded.

Reaching for the door she turned to thank him. He raised both hands up gesturing for a hug and asked her if it was okay.

"A holy hug," he said.

Not sure what to do, she nodded, and he took her into his arms. He smelled so good she thought. When she tried to pull away, stepping back from him he pulled her in tighter.

He whispered into her ear, "You are a precious angel. I have watched you and waited for you for so long. There is so much that I want to show you and do for you. Sara, you take my breath away and God has told me that you were meant for me to have and to hold."

Sara froze and stiffened. Pastor gently brushed her hair from around her face and over her shoulder and kissed her neck. She wanted to scream out, "No! Stop it! Please!" But when she opened her mouth nothing came out. He grabbed and lifted her chin and kissed her. She felt his warm tongue force its way into her mouth pushing passed the narrow crack between her upper and lower teeth. His tongue felt thick, threatening, and demanding. Having never been kissed by a man, she was not sure how to respond. Confusion, fear, and a deep sense of guilt engulfed and continued to paralyze her. He guided her to the side of his desk and pushed her onto it. He was not violent; he was forceful and determined.

SPIRITUAL WICKEDNESS IN HIGH PLACES

Feeling a sharp pain sticking her in the back she tried to move but the weight of his arm across her chest pinned her to the desk. Looking up she noticed the Creation of Adam by Michelangelo painted on the ceiling. The hand of God, reaching out to touch the hand of man and she wondered where her God was. Maybe, just maybe if she focused on that painting, he would once again save her. She did not cry, she did not fight, she did not move. His mouth was all over her. First her mouth, then her neck. He stood up, gathered her skirt around her waist and pulled at her panties until they began to give way, leaving her hips and thighs. As she felt his warm mouth and tongue on her then in her, she tightened her muscles, not daring to move. As he firmly grabbed the inside of her knees, squeezing them until her legs relaxed, giving way to the pressure, Sara pulled her arms up covering her mouth at first then moving to her chest she crossed them, each hand grabbing a shoulder holding her heaving chest as she struggled to hold back the panic and hysteria fighting to burst forth. He didn't notice the tears rolling down her checks and into her ears; he didn't notice the vacant look clouding over her eyes. He didn't see the bewilderment and betrayal she felt as her body started to relax and respond. What he was doing felt good, in an odd way, it was different. She started to shake, angry with her body for turning on her. If she did not participate, she would not go to hell, she thought. But she did not say no, she did not try to stop him, she did not move. He stood over her smiling as he unbuckled his pants.

"Yeah, I knew you were ripe and ready. You belong to me. From now on, you are mine. God gave you to me. I have watched and waited over the years for you to ripen," he whispered, his voice tense as he fumbled with his zipper.

Sara closed her eyes and felt something inside of her start to pull and tear, she sobbed, deep and gasping but silent, drawing air deep into her lungs and baring down with every ounce of energy she had, her mouth stretched wide open, but only silence. She would not let him hear her scream but in her mind, she was screaming. He moved in and out of her, slowly, gently, not pushing too hard. It felt like forever, faster, slower, rougher, gentler over and over again he said, "You are mine; God gave you to me." His voice growing strained with each thrust. All at once he jerked and gasped, his movement stopped and he laid on top of her, kissed her neck then her mouth, ignoring her tears and said, "It is complete, you are mine, God gave you to me."

He stood, his weapon of choice wet and bloody. Never making eye contact with her. Now she was no longer a person but his property. Walking behind his desk, still exposed he opened a drawer, took out a handkerchief and wiped himself off. Sara could hear the zipper on his pants. She remained lifeless, staring at the ceiling and holding her breath, listening as he grunted and poured something to drink. Every sound amplified and deafening, drowning out her pain.

With the blood-stained handkerchief in hand, he walked to her and gently wiped her thighs and between her legs. He helped her to stand and pulled up her panties. He never noticed that something had broken in her. He thought he had only taken her virginity. She was ripe after all. He never saw that he had taken her innocence and shattered her faith. He told her that he wanted her to go home and take a warm bath. He said that he would see her in church Sunday.

"Sara," he said "I don't have to tell you to not speak of this to anyone. God selects his handmaidens for his servants. He has chosen you for me. We'll talk about this later and what I expect of you."

Searching her mind, her heart and her soul for something, a scripture, a song, anything to help, she slowly and timidly walked out of the office. In the midst of her darkness, her internal voice began a repetitious loop with each cycle the words drilled deeper and deeper into her soul. "She had caused God's man to do something so bad.

SPIRITUAL WICKEDNESS IN HIGH PLACES

She caused him to sin, she had sinned, she was bad." How would she ever tell Lady Rose what she had done. As she walked out of the back door hearing it close and latch behind her, blood trickling down her legs, she noticed the sun was hidden by dark clouds and it became crystal clear that this would be the last time that she would ever set foot in a church again.

Downward Spiral

It had been 3 months since Sara had set foot in the Church. Lady Rose had come by, but she told her mother that she was not feeling well and did not want to talk to her. Her mom was curious but decided not to question her daughter. She was glad to have Sara's full attention on helping her at home. She didn't like all of that church stuff anyway and she damn sure could not figure out why poor people kept giving their money to it. From what she could see, the church took but never gave anything back in return.

Pastor Stanfield showed up once. Her mother took one look at him and told him to get his trifling ass off her porch. It was on this day that her mother told her all about Pastor Stanfield. She said that Chris Stanfield was known for having a thing for young girls. His lust for them was well know before he became a high and mighty pastor. The entire town was aware that he and Rose constantly fought over it.

Apparently, Rose had caught him cheating several times. She had a daughter from a previous marriage and caught Chris in bed with her. Rose sent her daughter to Atlanta to stay with her mother, and Rose tried to kill him. Rumor had it that she gave him a ten-inch cut across his stomach opening it wide and spilling his guts all over the floor. He refused to press charges against her to keep her quiet about his weaknesses. It was after this incident that Elder Washburn approached them both at the hospital. No one knows what he said or did, but after that visit, Rose and Chris started attending church and became born again Christians. Now they are Pastor Stanfield and Lady Rose. "Yeah, right," her mother said. "Whatever is going on with you and these people, well, let it go Sara. You have graduated from school, it is a good time to move on," she warned her.

After graduation Sara got a job as a bank teller during the day and was working nights selling newspaper subscriptions by phone. Church and what happened to her continued to occupy her thoughts. It had been months since she had opened her Bible. It had become a symbol of pain, deception and hurt. It had morphed into a souvenir of a horrible experience. That constant reminder lost its place of prominence on the nightstand by her bed and now rested in the back of a dresser drawer. The voice that once brought her comfort and guidance had stopped talking to her. A new voice took up residence in her head. Like the previous tenant, it came from within and reminded her that she created the mess, and her troubles were her fault. During her frequent nightmares she tried to focus on the chain of events and asked herself, was it her skirt, her hair, the hug, holding hands, what, how, why did the Pastor do that to her? Although she remained silent about what happened, she endured a grief that became a subtext to everything.

Sleep was never the same since that fateful day. She tossed and turned all night, to be pulled from the turmoil of sleep by her alarm's chirping. She couldn't even remember what it meant or felt like to be rested. Some mornings, she wondered if not sleeping would be better for her and asked herself over and over again, why would God give her to him and what does that mean? Why did her heart hurt and why did she feel so lost? Lately she not only relived what happened during her dreams but played the events over and over in her mind whenever she was alone. Each morning she rose slowly and reluctantly and sleepily made her way down the hall to the bathroom. Sara kept her eyes tightly shut so she wouldn't feel the burn of the light or look at herself in the mirror. Sara had lost ten pounds since the rape. Her appetite was gone and when she did eat, everything was tasteless. Her mouth was constantly dry, and she was lightheaded all the time. Her mom thought it was the summer flu, but Sara suspected it was the hot weather. "You know, that is the worst kind of sick - summer flu and colds," her mother would say.

Sara powered through her showered and slowly slipped into her clothes. The smallest decisions took extra effort. She was having trouble trying to decide between flat shoes or pumps. Noting the time, she quickly decided on the flats, determined to start her day on schedule. Lately even running a minute late could throw her whole day off. The hallway was oddly quiet, indicating that she was not the only one having trouble getting out of bed. She hurried down the hall, knocking on her siblings doors on her way to the kitchen. Determine to keep her positive momentum going Sara started brewing a pot of coffee for her mother and began pulling out milk, eggs, flour and other ingredients that go into making pancakes. She slowly mixed together the dry ingredients trying not to get anything on her clothes, stopping only for a second to wrap an apron around her waist before mixing the milk, eggs and vanilla then adding them to make a thick batter. While folding the mixture over and over she began feeling sick and closed her eyes and took three deep breaths. Her stomach clenched as the pancakes sizzled against the hot gray griddle. Pushing down the urge to give into an illness, she was determined to power through this "summer flu."

A few minutes later, Sara was brushing through her sister's hair, pulling the soft, tight curls into two afro puffs on either side of the little girl's head. As soon as she finished, she moved on to putting homework papers in backpacks. Mornings were like this, drowsy and fast-paced. Every movement was carried out on auto pilot and Sara only fully engaged as she waved goodbye to the departing school bus.

SPIRITUAL WICKEDNESS IN HIGH PLACES

Head down and determined to stay on schedule she returned to the kitchen to grab her purse. The square window in the door was draped with white curtains covered in a floral print. The space between the valance and the lower panels displayed just enough of a gap to see into the kitchen if she held her head up and slightly stretched upward. Jen was in the kitchen, nibbling on a pancake as if it were a slice of bread and sipping the coffee Sara made earlier. They acknowledged each other with a curt nod as she brushed past her mother to collect her purse and sweater. Noticing a ketchup stain on the sweater, she sighed in frustration and exchanged if for a light windbreaker. Hesitating briefly in the hallway and taking a deep breath she steadied herself and like a runner pushing off the block, she rushed into the kitchen with a single focus of making it through the back door before her mother uttered a word. To her great disappointment her mother was standing between her and the door, arms crossed and ready to engage.

"You got the kids off to school pretty fast today," her mother noted. Leaning over the counter, she glanced over her shoulder as Sara started to move towards the door. "Ah, don't move. You have time to eat something." She asked.

Jen stood up and pointed to a plate of pancakes and sliced strawberries garnished with a dollop of cool whip. Sara got it. She understood that this was her mom's way of showing her that she cared and loved her which made it all the harder for her to turn it down. Not wanting to hurt her mother's feeling but afraid that one bite might send her running into the bathroom she responded, "I'm good, not much of an appetite lately. Ma, I'm late and I have a granola bar in my purse." She wasn't exactly lying but she knew that, despite implying she would eat the granola bar, she wouldn't let, much if anything past her lips until dinner. Lately everything made her sick, and she had too much to get done today.

"Still down with that flu, hm?" her mother asked.

"I'm fine," Sara responded. She couldn't fake a smile with her mother so she figured a change of subject would do just as well. "Hey, don't forget it's grocery day so I'm taking the car. Anything more to add to the list?"

Jen shook her head.

"Okay. See you later." Sara quickly exited the house, the curtains fluttered under the rush of wind cause by the swiftly closing door. Shrugging off her mother's concern she stopped, lifted her chin to the morning sun and relished the cool breeze gently brushing her face and seemingly settling her stomach. As if on cue she began to relax.

Their gold Buick LeSabre was oddly parked in its usual place between the back door and the garage. Sara noticed the parked car was angled across the driveway and the driver's window was down. A tinge of guilt moved through her and touched her heart. She immediately understood why it had been left this way. This was the third time in a week that her mother had returned home from work late, exhausted and moving on auto pilot. An emotional struggle ensued within her, a battle between her mind and her heart. Her mind reminded her of the guilt of her rape while her heart pushed her to have compassion for her mother. Neither winning as she resisted a fleeting urge to pray and settled on the neutral place, indifference. Backing the car out of the driveway she took an alternate, indirect way to Wilts Grocery store, taking care to avoid driving past the church and hoping that she wouldn't run into any of its members while she shopped. Determined to gain control of her emotions and salvage the rest of the day, she turned her attention to shopping and how much she enjoyed stocking up and making sure everyone's favorite snack made it into the cart.

Pulling into the parking lot Sara noticed that only a few cars were present, none of which were familiar to her. Choosing a spot three

SPIRITUAL WICKEDNESS IN HIGH PLACES

spaces away from the door she carefully guided the car into the empty space and released the steering wheel feeling somewhat relieved as her nerves began to settle. It was stressful to constantly be on the lookout for Pastor Stanfield or Lady Rose. Drawing in a deep breath and bracing herself, she took another quick glance around the parking lot, taking care to note if anyone was watching, Sara left the car keeping her head down she grabbed a cart and walked briskly toward the entrance.

There were a lot of shopping carts in the parking lot, which seemed odd since they were normally kept inside. Entering the store, she immediately understood why they were outside. It was stock day. Every aisle was filled with boxes, some opened and partially empty and others completely empty laid discarded off to each side. "Whelp, this ought to be interesting," she thought. Committed to completing her task she plowed through, maneuvering around each obstacle. The boxes proved to be distracting enough to make shopping more difficult. On a normal day it only took one pass down each aisle, today it took three trips and constantly checking and crossing items off of the shopping list. Looking over the shopping list for the last time, Sara noticed that only one item remained: potato chips, three bags one barbecue, one plain with ridges and the third cheddar cheese. She pushed the cart loaded to the brim with groceries and headed for the snack aisle. Rounding the corner, leaning into the heavy cart as she pushed her world began to twist and turn. Overcome with dizziness, she stumbled and reached out grabbing a stack of boxes to steady herself. A small whimper escaped Sara's lips.

Mr. Wilts emerged from behind a stack of boxes. He had gone unnoticed earlier as he watch her erratic shopping, jumping between aisles, only to return a second and sometimes third time.

"Are you okay, Sara?" he asked. "Here, let me help you." He took her by the arm and guided her to a section of empty shelving to lean against until the dizziness passed. "There you go." His smile was kind as he stood in front of her.

"Yes, Mr. Wilts, I'm fine. It's all this heat, you know. Just thirsty," Sara told him. Regaining her balance, she stood and walked towards her cart. To her dismay, Mr. Wilts trailed behind her. "I really am fine, Mr. Wilts" she said speaking to him over her right shoulder.

He stopped briefly and grabbed a bottle of warm water and handed it to her, he replied, "Here, drink this."

"Thank you." She removed the cap and raised the bottle to her mouth, her hand trembling ever so slightly. It unnerved her. As she took a long drink, her eyes barely open, she peeked through the slits to see if Mr. Wilts was watching her. Seeing that his gaze never left her, she swallowed, let out a sigh and promised him that she was feeling much better. Mr. Wilts returned to stocking shelves but kept a watchful eye on her until he heard the bell next to the cash register ring alerting him to an impatient customer ready to check out.

Mr. Wilts was at the checkout counter finishing up with a customer when Sara arrived. Sara waited and watched him handle the transaction with ease, ringing up the groceries, bagging and placing them into the cart. When he finished, he executed his ritual of appreciation, to demonstrate his commitment to each customer. Mr. Wilts turned and smiled before extending his hand out for a handshake. And as the customer left, he called each of them by name and thanked them for their business.

His attention then turned to Sara who had been busy placing items from her cart to the conveyor belt he told her, "You should've asked for one of the boys in the back to come help you with all of this."

Sara chuckled as she responded. "I can handle it, Mr. Wilts. Besides, there will be plenty of help when I get home.'

SPIRITUAL WICKEDNESS IN HIGH PLACES

As he was ringing up her groceries his wife, Betty, came from the back of the store. She was known to have a mean streak but no matter how loud she barked at you, she always winked to let you know that she would not bite. But that bark could scare you to death if you didn't know her. She was a short round lady with a tight nappy afro. Ms. Betty baked all of the store's cakes, cookies, pies, and breads fresh each day. She was easy to pick out because she always wore a white chef's hat and matching apron. Sara thought she should change the tall hat for a hair net since it brought attention to her face and the large mole that set prominently on the right side of her nose. Betty approached the cash register and stood behind Mr. Wilts and began bagging the groceries. She looked at Sara, smiled and said, "Hey, little girl" and not waiting on a response, resumed bagging groceries. Glancing back and forth between watching the balance steadily increase and Betty effortlessly placing items in the bag as if she were putting together a jigsaw puzzle, she saw Betty reach into her apron pocket and pulled out a small package and drop it into one of the bags.

"Ms. Betty, what is that?" Sara asked.

"Just a little gift, baby, girl to girl. If you don't want it, bring it back," she said with a nod and a wink. With her mission accomplished, she turned on her heels and walked off singing, "I've got a feelin, everything's gonna be all right. Oh, oh, oh, I've got a feelin everything's gonna be alright, be alright, be alright, be alright!"

Sara and Mr. Wilts both watched her walk away singing and swaying as she raised her right arm upwards.

Mr. Wilts shook his head. "Ms. Betty is a strange bird sometimes, but I love her. I'm sure that her surprise is a late graduation gift," he said.

Sara nodded and smiled. "How thoughtful and sweet. You guys did not have to do that, but thank you," she said.

"Well, that was all her but if you like it, I'll take the credit for it!" he chuckled.

After Sara paid him, he helped her place the bags into her cart and insisted on helping her load them into the car. Not having the energy to argue with him, she nodded in agreement and led the way to the car. As with all of his customers he thanked her for shopping at his store and walking away reminded her of the graduation gift in the bag

Groceries loaded into the back seat and feeling pretty accomplished she slid into the car, put the key in the ignition and started the engine. With the car in reverse, she started backing up, her right arm along the top of the bench style seat as she stretched to look out the back window, careful not to hit anything. Her shift at the bank didn't start until 10:00 am which gave her another hour to get home, unload the car and put the food away. The car abruptly came to a halt as she instinctively pressed the break. Looking at the bags she wondered what was in the gift box. Sara was going to wait until she got home to find out, but her curiosity got the best of her. She put the car in park and reached over the front seat into one of the bags feeling around for the gift. Finding it by touch was turning out to be harder than she realized since the gift was wrapped in plain white paper and did not have a bow. Not finding it in the first bag she turned completely around and leaned over the seat, with her butt in the air nearly touching the roof, she searched each bag until she found it. With it in hand she quickly turned around, falling into the front seat. She was lightheaded and dizzy again but this time it was clearly due to all of the blood rushing to her head while she searched. Looking at the wrapping she noticed that there was a note written on it.

"Sweet Sara, my mama used to say that still water ran deep, so keep an eye on the quiet ones. I know that you are a good girl, but even good girls make

SPIRITUAL WICKEDNESS IN HIGH PLACES

mistakes. I am always here to listen and help if you need someone to confide in. ~ Ms. Betty"

A mistake, could she possibly know about Pastor Stanfield, what in the world and what an odd thing to say she thought tearing the wrapping away from the box. A puzzled look formed on Sara's face as she examined the contents. As the realization of what it could mean became clearer, she began to gasp. Feeling her chest tighten she dropped the gift into her lap and fumbled around desperately trying to open the car door. Her groping hand finally finding the handle, she barely opened the door in time, emptying the contents of her stomach, on the pavement and the side of the car. Stepping over the vomit, she exited the car, searching for a breath of fresh air. Her face sweaty and her nostrils filled with the stench she nervously glanced around to see if anyone was watching her. Looking down at the puddle of bile she noticed the box partially covered in puke. Her first instinct was to step over it, get into the car and leave, however she picked it up and walked over to a trash can sitting next to the entrance of the store. Holding onto a corner of the box, she reached inside of the trash and pulled out a piece of paper and slowly wiped it clean. Placing the box on the seat next to her, she started the car and backed out of the parking space. Pulling slowly out of the lot, she glanced at the box and knew that she needed to come to terms with it and what it meant; but not today. She reached over and grabbed the pregnancy test, stuffing it into her purse and pushing it to the back of her mind was an act of defiance, however the war in her mind had begun to rage, the seed was planted and all she could think about was the box.

On the drive home, Sara decided that she was not pregnant. It just wasn't possible. Pastor Stanfield had only touched her that one time. But maybe Ms. Betty knew something, why else would she give her a pregnancy test. During their brief interaction in the store, Ms. Betty had offered her a sample of her freshly baked pecan pie and seemed both baffled and offended when she turned it down. She had twisted her face, frowned and said "Little girl, nobody, and I mean *nobody* turns down my pies. It just ain't natural!"

Sara shrugged and sheepishly said, "Sorry, Ms. Betty" and walked away. "Could it be that there is some old wives tale about pregnancy and pie," she dared to consider or was Ms. Betty so offended that this was her way of getting back at her. Regardless, the test presented her with a serious problem and if it is possible, it was an indication that her simple life was becoming more complicated. At the moment, she just did not have the energy or the nerve to deal with it.

A week later, standing in her room with the box in hand, turning it over and over she decided to take the test. Trying to avoid the others she gently opened her bedroom door and looked down the hall to make sure no one was around. The house seemed quiet and seeing no one, she tucked the box into her hip pant pocket, pulled her shirt over it and eased down the hallway to the bathroom. Locking the door behind her and turning on the radio, she sat on the side of the bathtub, opened the box, and pulled out a long white stick with a pink cap on it. The instructions directed her to hold the tip of the stick under a urine stream and do it first thing in the morning. It was 2:00 o'clock in the afternoon. Not wanting to wait and hoping that taking it later in the day would lead to a negative result she decided to go ahead and take the test.

The instructions said to pee on the stick, shake off the excess urine and wait two minutes for the results. The center of the stick would reveal the answer in words. Sara thought if it just says yes or no, what does that mean? Yes, could mean, yes you are not pregnant, and no could mean, no you are pregnant. The mental gymnastics brought on by denial had started before one drop of urine hit the test. Sitting on the toilet she held the stick between her legs and peed. Her knees bounced up and down as her anxiety grew stronger with each passing second. She continued to pee on the stick until she stopped. Pulling it from between her legs, she glanced at the results window and immediately saw the word: "Pregnant."

Shaking the stick, she looked again, and the terrifying yet telling word remained. Still sitting on the toilet, she reached over to the sink and ran warm water over it, but the word "pregnant" remained boldly centered in the middle of the little oval window, the word confronted her, undeniable and unrelenting. Placing her head in her lap, she started to tremble and wept. Giving way to despair and hopelessness her body slid to the floor, the cool tiles provided little comfort. Lying there with her panties pooled around her ankles, ass exposed and her mind racing she felt completely lost.

"No one could know this," she thought, without considering how she could possibly keep it a secret.

In moments like these, emotions give way to ridiculous and unrecoverable decisions. For now, an answer to her dilemma which she could not fully understand or define seemed out of reach. There was a reluctance in the way she pushed herself off the floor and turned to face her reflection in the mirror. It wasn't the puffiness of her face or the tear-stained cheeks that caught her attention, but the profound sadness in her eyes. She looked away, glancing at the floor and the panties which remained around her ankles as if they were shackles that anchored her to the floor. She slowly pulled them and her pants up around her waist and gently opened the bathroom door. Cautiously peeking up and down the hallway in search of any oncoming traffic, she let out an audible sigh of relief and quietly returned to her room where she hid the box and test stick in her purse. Not knowing what to do next or where to go she walked to a corner of the room and with her back against the wall, slid to the floor and grabbed her knees pulling them tightly to her chest. Wondering if things could get any worse, she remembered the Pastor had said that she belonged to him. As he raped her, she could hear him praying and speaking in tongues. He alternated between the language of angels and the words of man, telling her that she belonged to him. At that moment, for better or worse, she decided that she had to tell him and show him the test. After all he was God's man. He would know what to do.

Submit And Obey

It was a typical Wednesday afternoon for Pastor Stanfield. He faithfully visited those in the hospital in the morning and afterwards met Rose at Bella's Soul Food Diner for lunch promptly at 11:30. They had a special booth near the back of the room close to the kitchen. Everyone in town ate at least breakfast, lunch or dinner at Bella's. Years ago, the original Italian owners had converted three old train box cars into a diner and served the best home-made pasta and pastries in northern Indiana. As the Black community continued to grow and expand north of the tracks, they sold it and relocated further north. Kizzy Johns purchased it and named it Bella's. It didn't take long for the community to stop referring to her as Kizzy and start calling her Bella. She was a shrewd businesswoman and one hell of a cook. She realized that she could catch the church folk for a meal but needed something a little looser and steamier for the night crowd. About a year after opening Bella's and capturing the stomachs of the righteous, she opened Montel's Bar at 6th and Indiana and captured the hearts of the sinners.

Bella knew Chris and Rose when they were running the street and frequenting Montel's. She often bragged about how they were the example of what God can do for a person. Of course, it helped that she also considered him a good-looking man and Pastor always enjoyed being the center of attention. Afterall he had to show the young men how to treat their helpmate and he needed the young women to see how his wife loved to cater to him.

Entering the diner, he could see the top of Rose's head. She never left him waiting and dutifully sat patiently awaiting his arrival. As he approached the booth, he could see that Rose had ordered his food and a cup of coffee. He reached for her hand, lifted it to his lips and kissed it. She smiled and said, "Pastor, we need to talk,". He loved to hear her call him that but wondered what she wanted and if she was going to try and butter him up to say yes to a big request, whatever that might be.

"Can I at least take a seat first?" he asked.

"My apologies, I have been anxious to talk to you. I waited up for you last night, but fell asleep before you came in," she responded.

"Well, what could be that important Rose? I mean seriously, what on earth can be so important that you felt the need to wait up for me?", he demanded.

Rose could feel his frustration mounting and could tell by the tone of his voice that he was annoyed. However, she felt that she needed to tell him what she had overheard some of the deacons discussing.

'Umm, I'm sorry," she stammered, "I just thought that you would want to know that yesterday, when I was vacuuming the hallway, Deacon Johnson stepped out of his office and asked that I stop and come back later. He said the noise was distracting them from a meeting he was holding with the newly appointed deacons. Of course, I agreed. As I was unplugging and wrapping the cord, I overheard him telling the others how to manipulate people to get more money out of them during the offering. He said they should encourage the congregants to give their money and tell them not to worry about how their bills got paid. He said if they gave, God would miraculously pay the bills and if God didn't it was because they were not praying and fasting enough." Rose's voice started out as a whisper but got louder and louder as she told the story. It was clear to those who could not hear the conversation that she was upset.

"My Pastor, this is just wrong, you have to stop them!" she demanded, slamming her fist onto the table.

Chris snapped at her. "Lower your voice foolish woman! This is not acceptable, eavesdropping on Deacon Johnson. What is wrong with you?" he asked.

Rose was shocked and confused. Noticing heads turning to see what was going on, she could not believe that he was hushing and chastising her so publicly. Chris continued scolding her.

"The church's money is none of your business. How dare you step out of your place and question the direction of a man of God? I would suggest that you shut your mouth and forget what you think you overheard. Pray for forgiveness woman!" he demanded, his eyes never leaving hers, his smile never leaving his lips as he quietly delivered his tongue lashing. Stopping long enough to acknowledge the waitress with a "Bless you sister" as she stopped to refresh their drinks.

Rose's face conveyed her embarrassment. She lowered her head and continued eating the rest of her meal in silence as she thought about their past and how much she had given of herself to serve God. Since that dreadful day when she had caught him having sex with her daughter Emily and tried to kill him, their life had drastically changed.

The thought of Chris touching her daughter and the anger of not being enough of a woman for him had sent her into a rage. She ran into the kitchen and grabbed a carving knife. Chris had run after her, calling her name over and over again. When he came up behind her and placed his hands on her shoulders, leaning in and kissing her neck, she turned and ran the knife across his abdomen, slicing him open. She had taken a step back to watch him fall. His eyes wide and his mouth gapping as the shock registered on his face. It seemed to take a minute before his brain signaled him that it hurt. Instinctually his hands grabbed his side, his intestines bubbled through his fingers and he screamed as he slid to the floor, fighting to hold his bowels inside of himself. As she spit on him, she looked up to find her daughter standing in the doorway, frozen with her hands over her mouth.

Realizing what she had done, Rose hid the knife and called 911. She warned her daughter to not say a word. Admonishing her for making advances and flirting with Chris. Emily held back her tears until she heard her mother's second phone call. It was to her grandmother in Atlanta. Her mother was sending her away. That news made her cry. Rose knew that her daughter was beautiful and immature. She had imagined her becoming a teen mother, but not her having sex with her stepfather. The only way she could protect her was to send her away and her only regret was that she had not done it sooner.

As Chris laid in his hospital bed, rumors swirled around the city that someone had broken into their home and tried to rob him; a rumor that he and Rose started. Rose sat by his bed day and night worried that an infection would set in and she would have to hide a murder instead of an assault.

After several days in the hospital, Elder Washburn paid them a visit. He asked Rose to leave them for a minute so he could talk to Chris. He watched her leave the hospital room and waited for the door to swing shut behind her. He then turned his attention to Chris and called out to him.

"Christopher," he said, "Son we need to talk and please forgive me for getting right to the point, but I need to speak my mind before your wife returns. I'm aware that you have a special taste for tender meat. Some may see your desires as sin, I prefer to call them, simply, preferences. Seeing your current situation, I imagine that it has caught up with you." Chris remained silent. He was not a sucker and in no way would he confirm anything for this man. Elder Washington continued.

"God understands the weaknesses of man. That's why the bible says that all things are permissible to those of us who follow Jesus, they are just not always expedient. Might I point out that the way you are going about it definitely isn't expedient. You can't control these desires within. Hell, none of us can. You need the help of the Lord and the support of the brothers in the church. We all have our little indiscretions. But together we look out for one another," pausing for effect now that he had Chris' attention. He continued, " Now the church provides a perfect shopping mall, shall I say. The women come in all shapes, sizes and ages. Some of them we have to groom and others we have to break. Either way, their weaknesses and desires, just being the seductive creatures that they are, requires us to control them. The bible is noticeably clear about this."

Chris was not sure what exactly the aging pastor was saying to him. Fearful of interpreting the conversation wrong or sounding like a fool from all of the pain medication he was on, he remained silent. Instinctually he looked towards the door to see if Rose had reentered the room. Pastor Washburn, following his eyes, turned to look as well. Seeing that they were still alone, he continued.

"Now through the brotherhood, we look out for each other. We each stay in our own lane and the first to stake his claim, well that woman or girl, belongs to him and him alone. All of the brothers know that particular woman is hands off to them. You understand?" Chris shook his head no and remained silent.

"There is more to the brotherhood but until you join, well let's just say the rest shall remain a mystery. I'm giving you an opportunity to have your desires fulfilled and your behaviors hidden." He waited a few seconds and asked Chris, "Are you ready son?"

At first Chris was speechless. But there was something powerful about this man and he wanted it for himself. "Ready for what? You trying to run some hustle on me old man?" Chris asked.

"Why, to accept Jesus as your Lord and Savior son and to teach you the ultimate hustle" Elder Washington replied with a slight smile.

"And my wife?" Chris asked.

"Don't worry about her. We will shape her into the servant she was designed to be. Seems to me like she is pretty strong willed. She will become the example for other young women to follow. Especially as you move into a new house and she starts to receive nice things. My wife, Brenda, was the same way but through my teachings, she has seen that the more she serves me and endures with a glad heart, the more pleasing she is to God. Under Brenda's tutoring Rose will come around, trust me," he assured him.

"Ok, what do I need to do?" Chris asked.

"Let's get Rose back in here. Watch and learn young blood. Watch and learn," he responded.

Elder Washburn walked to the door and looked into the hallway. Rose was walking towards him with a cup of coffee in one hand and a small brown bag in the other. She walked with authority and confidence, her back straight and her head held high. As she approached the door she wondered if Chris was ok and why the Elder was standing there obviously looking for her. Maybe he had talked some sense into Chris. After all, being raised in the Evangelical church as a child, she always held a little guild for living so wildly. She also quietly thanked God that she had not killed Chris. She loved him and was in a constant state of confusion as to why she seemed to never be enough for him. Afterall, she still turned men's heads as she walked by. She was young, beautiful and smart. Not like her daughter who had a woman's body, full lips and hips, flat stomach, a small waist and long curly hair. Yet simple minded as they come. She really could not blame Chris for sleeping with her. Emily was coming into her own sexuality and was a big flirt but lacked the understanding of the danger that came with it. "Mama will keep her straight. She is better off in Georgia anyway." She thought.

"Elder Washington, is Chris ok?" Rose asked.

"Of course, daughter, he replied. "I just need to speak with the both of you. Come on inside."

Rose entered the room and walked over to the far side of Chris' bed. She took his hand and gave him a questioning look. She hoped that he had not opened up and told the Elder everything. Chris smiled and squeezed her hand. Rose turned her attention to the Elder who was now standing at the foot of the bed. He cleared his throat and began his sales pitch.

"Well now," he began, " you both are very blessed. I thank God for keeping you safe Rose, and for sparing your life Chris. A tinge of guilt entered Rose's heart, and she prayed that Chris had not betrayed her.

"You two are not members of my church, but God told me to come and see you both today. He said that you were lost and tired. He wanted me to ask if you would live for him after all he has done for the both of you. Sin is a heavy burden, are you not tired of the load you carry? Don't you want the peace that only he can give?"

The guilt Rose had begun to feel, quickly converted to anger. How dare this man show up acting holy and try to manipulate them into joining his church. She guessed he would ask for their tithes next. As she opened her mouth to give him a piece of her mind, Chris squeezed her hand and said, "Yes Elder, I am tired. I love my wife and have hurt her so much over the years. I want to chance to become the husband she needs and the friend she has not had in a very long time."

Rose's mouth dropped wide open. She tilted her head to the side and looked at her husband, wondering if the medication was too strong. Becoming suspicious she considered what in the hell was going on. Chris, still holding her hand, looked at her and nodded. She noticed his eyes watering. And in that moment, she remembered the intimacy they use to have and longed for it one again. If this is what he wants, if this brings her husband back to her, then she would follow him.

Her gazed locked in on her husband, she asked the elder what they needed to do.

"Accept Jesus right now, start attending church and open your heart to your new family," he replied.

After that day, both of them because dedicated to the church. Chris went to bible study with the men's group and eventually because a deacon, then Associate Pastor and finally the Pastor. Rose settled into the ladies' group and attended classes lead by Sister Brenda. She came to understand that she needed to serve her husband. She learned that a woman in the church should remain silent unless asked to speak.

Chris became exceedingly kind. He would listen to her and sometimes, when he was not too tired, he would make love to her. Gentle, slow, deliberate. She felt like she was all that mattered when he touched her. For that she lost herself in him. She kept her head down and stayed busy in the church. There were times, at least three days a week when he arrived home late and ignored her. A few times she thought she smelled alcohol, but she never questioned him. He had a lot of responsibilities. Now as Pastor, he carried everyone's problems on his shoulders.

SPIRITUAL WICKEDNESS IN HIGH PLACES

The tinkling sound of fresh tea being poured into her glass pulled her from the grasp of her memories. She looked at Chris who was also deep in thought and hoped that his displeasure with her would not last. His attention was on his plate of food as he never looked up at her while he ate his meal. She noticed a slight smile etch its way across his face.

Chris at his lunch in silence. He was pleased that Rose felt wounded and was silently licking them. He thought about how his world had changed for the better and how he had found his home in the church and it made him smile. Being a Deacon was ok and the role of Associate Pastor had its rewards, but the grand prize was being The Pastor. To get there he spent months absorbing the bible and setting his sights on playing the game. The Brotherhood admired his street smarts and ability to raise money for the church. Even though he was married, the women all secretly held crushes on him. All he needed to do was deliver a fiery sermon and break out into song. On cue, he would come from behind the pulpit and touch their hands, look into their eyes and they would empty their purses. He only approached the single women. The ones who obviously needed and desired a man's attention.

On one occasion, the deacons told him that one woman had placed her electric bill with cash in it into the offering basket. When asked what they should do Chris advised, "Take the money and pay her bill. She will swear it was a miracle from God and the next time we will get more out of her. That will be the money that we keep and as an added bonus she'll testify about her miracle and encourage others to give as well! Amen!"

"Amen!" they responded.

Chris' memory next flashed on his first men's group meeting. He and Rose had been members for two months when Elder Washburn told him that he was ready to move to the next level and invited him to a meeting of the "The Brotherhood". The meeting was held at Associate Pastor Calvin Peterson's place, a two-story farmhouse with a full finished basement located near the village of Cass Michigan. The house was at least seven thousand square feet with a porch that wrapped around the entire structure. It was nestled in the middle of 20 wooded acres. Cass was a 30-minute drive north of Elkhart. Calvin's house was another 10 minutes northwest of the city limits. Chris could tell from all of the parked cars that he was the last to arrive. Not knowing what to expect, he brought his bible along with him. With it in hand he was ready to hear about this brotherhood. As he approached the porch, Calvin opened the door and greeted him.

"Welcome Chris, I'm so glad that you decided to join us tonight, come on inside," he said.

Chris smiled and entered the home. It was modestly furnished and very neat. It appeared as if no one else lived there. Calvin asked him what he would like to drink. Feeling unsure of the boundaries he asked for a coke. Calvin laughed and told him that he would take the liberty to add a little rum to his drink. He excused himself and left the room, returning in a few seconds with his rum and coke. Chris took the drink, nodded and consumed a long sip. He had to admit that he was a little nervous and the drink would help to settle his nerves. Calvin waited for Chris to finish his second sip and led the way into what appeared to be his library. There were bookshelves, loaded with books that spanned from the ceiling to the floor. Across the room and framed by more bookshelves was a second door. He followed Calvin through the doorway and into an open stairway that was wide enough for the both of them to comfortably walk down the steps side by side. As they were nearing the last step, Chris could hear the faint sound of music playing. He noticed large windowless wood doors on the right and the left of the stairs. They were made of solid cherry with bronze handles. Each door had a peep hole. Calvin turned to Chris and said, "We will always start out our meetings on the right, and as the night goes on and you feel the need for more privacy, well let's just say that the door on the left is the devil's playground."

Calvin opened the door on the right, and they entered a large room. It reminded Chris of an old 1930's smoking lounge. The furniture was overstuffed burgundy leather chairs and sofas. The backs were tufted, and the frames were accented by gold studs. The lights were dim, and the music was a light jazz. It was a man's room, full of strength and power. The walls were papered in red, gold and green thin stripped patterns. The carpet was sculpted and dark green. At the far end of the room was a long bar. It had a pillar at each end, a long mirror stretched across the wall behind it and lined with glass shelves full of expensive bottles of alcohol resting on each shelf. A man, who appeared to be in his early 20s, was tending bar. He was introduced as Jason and smiled as he nodded in his direction. He quickly turned his attention back to the bar and wiping off the bottles on the shelf. Little did he know, that from this angel, Jason could watch everyone. As his environment began to sink in, Chris could not help but wonder what he had gotten into.

Looking around the room, he noticed seven preachers from neighboring churches and five deacons. All of the mega church pastors were there and a few of the old small storefront churches were represented as well. The men all wore black suits and clergy collars. Some were smoking cigars and all of them has a drink in their hand. Calvin walked Chris around the room and made introductions. The men welcomed him and offered their support with whatever he may need in his new capacity at the church. At least three of the men had to be in their late 80's or early 90's. All were Black and all held positions of authority and respect in the community.

While Chris was sizing everyone up, Calvin interrupted his thoughts by calling the meeting to order. The first item on the agenda was reciting the Brotherhood's oath. He asked all of the brothers to repeat after him.

"We stand together as one mind, one body, with one desire to uphold our promise to the Brotherhood and to protect it at all costs. We pledge to carry its secrets to our graves as we admire God's handiwork and partake in it. Our reward is the blessing of the first fruits which are rightfully ours. We will not covet that which is claimed by our brother. For what is his, is his, what is mine is mine and what is ours, is ours. To the Brotherhood!" they chanted raising their glasses in the air and toasting each other.

The next item on the agenda was welcoming the new member. Chris learned that the brotherhood must always remain at 13 members. He counted 12 people in the room and knew he would become the 13th member. Elder Washburn proudly boasted that he had recruited Chris and was looking forward to having someone with his similar tastes, who was also growing the coffers of the church, becoming active in the Brotherhood. "He is quite the ladies' man to boot!", he chuckled as he coughed between laughing and choking on his cigar. "Some of us are getting old and we must ensure that the brotherhood continues on!" he said. The other men yelled "here! here!" erupting in applause.

Elder Washburn was feisty and restless. He wanted to show Chris the true benefit of the Brotherhood. He looked at Calvin and said "Calvin, I think I want to skip dinner and just have dessert tonight!"

Calvin rolled his eyes and shook his head. "Old man, all of that sugar is going to be the death of you. Let's have dinner first, you need to keep your strength up," he laughed.

The old man looked over the rim of his glass and firmly said, "We will start with dessert tonight, understood?"

SPIRITUAL WICKEDNESS IN HIGH PLACES

Nodding, Calvin turned to the others, "Gentlemen, can I have your attention please. Elder wants to start with dessert first to night. Shall we move into the desert room?" he asked as he pushed a button on the wall near the door. Everyone stood in agreement and with drinks in hand, followed Calvin across the hall.

Entering the room, a wide toothy grin slowly appeared on Chris' face and his pants grew a little tighter. Lined up, in the nude were 13 young women, who appeared to range in age between 16-23. Calvin turned to face the men and said, "As our newest member, Brother Chris will get to choose first," Chris walked over to the 16-year-old and took her by the hand. She did not pull away or resist but smiled at him. He leaned over and gently brushed her hair away from her ear and whispered, "You are mine."

Lost in their own thoughts, Chris and Rose silently finished their lunch. Chris was the first to break the silence, "Look, why don't you spend some time with Sister Brenda today. I am sure she will help you understand the importance in knowing how to stay in your place. Give her a call and see if you can drop by for a cup of coffee. I, on the other hand am headed to the Church. It is Wednesday and I need to prepare my sermon for this Sunday. I was thinking of preaching on the glory of a virtuous woman. What do you think?" he asked.

Rose looked up at him and with a tear rolling down her cheek she responded, "Yes my Pastor, forgive me. I think it's always helpful to be reminded."

"Good, Good. Now that's my girl. I will see you later on tonight, and darling be ready to receive your husband," he commanded.

He stood up, kissed her on the cheek and walked out of the diner. Rose watched as he left, greeting others and holding on a little too long to the hands of the women that offered them. She was torn. She loved her home and lifestyle. Having become accustomed to living well and having influence she felt nauseated, as her stomach churned and her heart raced, at the mere thought of ever having to give any of it up. For a few luxuries and privileges, she realized that she had lost the things she used to value the most, her voice and her strength. Maybe Sister Brenda could help her learn to forget who she used to be.

Betrayed

Sara waited under a large oak tree at the back of the church. It provided shade and allowed her to stay hidden from passing traffic. Pastor Stanfield arrived at the church on Wednesdays, promptly at 1:30 in the afternoon. She looked at her watch and it was 1:15. As each minute passed, she became more anxious. For the last several days, she played over in her mind how she would approach him and tell him about the pregnancy. Sara could not think of her situation, her pregnancy, in terms of being a mom. Unable to accept what was growing inside of her, she wondered if something conceived in violence and evil could ever be good. Not sure if the Pastor was good or evil, she needed to trust him.

Pastor Stanfield pulled into his parking spot at exactly 1:30. He placed the car in park and lowered the sun visor to look at himself in the mirror before getting out of the car. He knew he was a good-looking man. This town was his and he was God's gift to them, he thought as he gently ran his index finger over each eyebrow, smoothing them and winking at himself. Taking one last glance he flipped the visor up and reached for the door handle. As he opened the door, he quickly looked at the rearview mirror and caught a glimpse of someone pacing back and forth between the trees at the edge of the parking lot. Getting out of his car he placed his hand above his eyes to prevent the glare of the sun and focused his sight on the direction of the old Oak tree. Sara emerged from behind it. Half-elated and curious to hear why she was there, he walked over to her calling out her name. Sara panicked, forgetting everything she had planned to say and stared at him, eyes wide open, without blinking. He grabbed her by the shoulders and asked if she was alright. Sara nodded as he pulled her to him. She jerked away from him and blurted out "I'm pregnant!"

The Pastor took a step back from her and looked around the parking lot to see if anyone else was there. He rubbed his temples and shook his head back and forth as he thought. After what seemed to Sara to be an eternity, he grabbed her shoulders again and asked, "Is it mine? Are you sure? Who else knows about this?"

Sara did not know what to expect but she surely was not expecting all of the questions. Teetering between anger and fear she responded, "Yes, at least that is what the pregnancy test said, and I have not said anything to anyone. You asked me if it is yours, you know what you did to me, you know that I had never been with anyone, I…I… don't know what to do!"

The Pastor knew that he could not risk her creating a scene. He took her hands and bowed his head as if praying. Anyone watching would assume that this was someone coming to him for prayer.

With his head bowed he calmly said to her, "Everything is going to be okay. I am here for you, remember that you are mine. This is not the place to talk about this. How about dinner tonight? I can pick you up and we can drive over to South Bend and have a nice dinner and figure this out together. Sara can we do that?"

She nodded and answered "Yes."

Still holding her hands, he said, "I will pick you up tonight at 8:30. Meet me in the alley behind your house. We won't be gone long; I will have you home by midnight."

He dropped her hands, turned, and walked into the church.

SPIRITUAL WICKEDNESS IN HIGH PLACES

Sara walked home looking at the ground the entire way. She was so ashamed and confused. How in the world would he ever fix this and what did they need to figure out, she thought? Abortion is not an option. Her grandmother told her once that good girls had babies and bad girls didn't. Sara hoped that keeping the baby would help her earn God's forgiveness. She decided that after talking to the Pastor tonight, she was going to tell her mother. Her mom may be rough around the edges, but she was also a fighter and she would know exactly what to do. She was determined to tell her everything.

For the rest of the afternoon, Sara was nervous and could not focus. She had pulled several outfits together trying to decide on what to wear. She had laid out a white sundress but thought it was too informal, a skirt and an off the shoulder blouse and felt that it sent the wrong message, and a pair of slacks with a light sweater and flat shoes. She settled on slacks deciding that if he tried to rape her this time she would fight back.

At 8:30 she slipped out of the back door, taking care not to be noticed by her siblings, and quickly walked behind the garage and into the alley. Two houses away she noticed the Pastor's car. It was a Cadillac Escalade, black with tinted windows. She walked to the car and opened the front passenger door. Sitting behind the wheel was Calvin! Shocked, she asked, "Where is Pastor?"

Calvin looked at her and smiled. "Sister Sara, how wonderful it is to see you. Pastor asked me to pick you up and take you over to South Bend to meet with him. Consider me your personal Chauffeur for the night," he said.

Sara hesitated, a bad feeling started to consume her, all of her senses screamed at her to not go. Pushing feelings aside, she joined him in the front seat.

There was an awkward silence between them during the ride. She caught Calvin glancing over at her and felt that he knew her secret. She focused her attention on the houses they passed and the route they were talking. Twice Calvin tried to start a conversation with her, but she responded with one-word answers. Eventually he gave up, turned on gospel music and focused on driving.

Twenty minutes later Calvin pulled into a small parking lot next to a restaurant called Big Willey's Special Barbecue Joint. It was a small place that looked more like a bar than a restaurant. It was a green cement block building with a flat roof. The windows looked like they had never been cleaned. Painted across them were drawings of a pig, a plate with a slab of ribs, a basket of French fries and various pies. At some point the place probably looked nice, she thought, but tonight coupled with the filth and dim lights it was scary.

She looked at Calvin and said, "Pastor is here?"

Calvin responded, "Oh, so now you want to talk. Yeah girl, he is here. Go on inside now. He will be sitting in one of the booths on the right. He likes to be close to the kitchen. He is waiting for you, so hurry up. I will be here to take you back home when you're ready."

Sara put her phone in her purse. She studied Calvin trying to see if he was lying to her. Calvin looked into her eyes and said, "Go on now."

Sara eased out of the car and reluctantly walked towards the entrance.

Once inside it became obvious that Big Willey's was more of a bar than a restaurant. It was dimly lit, and it took a few seconds for her eyes to adjust. The bar was in the middle of the floor with seats on three sides. There were booths along one wall. The opposite side of the room was home to three pool tables. The place was dingy and smelled like smoke and beer. The booths had high backs and it was difficult to see if anyone was sitting in them. Hooks for coats hung along the sides of each one. Sara could not make out the color of the sticky floor. It was too dark to tell. She noticed that there were not many people in the place. At the front of the bar was a woman sitting alone smoking a cigar. She looked at Sara eyeing her from head to toe and acknowledged her with a nod. On the left side of the bar towards the back was a big muscular guy. He was standing with his arms crossed at his chest, talking with the bartender who was drying glasses. The big man stopped talking and looked at Sara. The bartender turned his attention to her as well and asked if he could help her. Before she could answer, he interrupted her and asked

"How old are you?"

Sara responded, "Nineteen."

"Look Miss, you have to be twenty-one to even come in here, so turn ya cute little ass around and get to steppin. Shoo chile, I ain't playin with ya, shoo!"

Pastor stood and interjected, "She belongs to me, Joey."

Joey saluted Pastor and went back to drying glasses.

Relieved, Sara walked towards the booth where Pastor sat, nervously counting each one as she passed. She stopped at the fifth booth in the back on the right side and stood beside it. The old red leather was ripped in places. The table had hot sauce, a small plastic red basket of wet wipes, a jar of pickled peppers, napkins and a salt and pepper shaker on it. The tabletop was wood and had scratches all over it. In several places, people had scratched names into it. Pastor motioned for her to sit down. "Hey Joey!" he yelled. "Bring me another Cognac on the rocks and bring my girl a glass of Moscato." Sara had never seen Pastor like this. He was wearing a pair of jeans, and a long sleeve white shirt. The cuffs of his shirt sleeves were folded up just below his forearm and he did not have on a tie. The collar was open revealing a gold cross and the soft curl of his chest hair. He was a handsome man, she thought.

Not knowing how to begin the conversation, she looked at him and waited. Joey brought the drinks to the table. She looked at him and before he could set her drink down, she raised her hand and said, "I am sorry, but I don't drink alcohol."

Joey looked at Pastor not sure what to do. Pastor responded, "It's okay, bring her a glass of ginger ale." Looking at Sara he asked her if that was ok and she nodded.

Joey said, "No problem, how about food? Y'all eating anything?"

"Man, you know it, bring me a full order of tips with some slaw and fries. Bring my girl Mama's famous pulled pork sandwich and some fries." Pastor responded. He looked at Sara as he ordered for her. She did not mind; she wasn't hungry anyway. She wanted to talk. Joey walked away leaving the two of them alone.

"Sara, I know we have something important to talk about. More important, you need to listen. At a time like this, you must trust me as you trust the Lord. You are my responsibility. I claimed you and showed my love for you in my office and told you that you belong to me," he said.

Sara leaned forward slightly and in a hushed voice said, "You raped me. I don't belong to you or to God. I belong to me."

Pastor looked at her. She noticed a vein along his jawline pulse as it tightened. He wanted to slap her for speaking to him in such a disrespectful way. But maintaining self-control was important. He would not let this woman forget her place.

"Ah, I do not think you understand," he said. "First, you are pregnant with my child. You will lower your voice and act like you are a virtuous Christian woman. Second, I told you that you belong to me.

I claimed you. That comes with responsibilities. I do not have any other children. I want this child, and I want you. I have been thinking about everything. Taking care of you and our baby is what is important to me. Now, I have made my decision and you will do what I asked you to do," he stated.

Reaching across the table he took Sara's hand. She pulled away from him. Confused, she was not sure what to do next. Part of her wanted to trust him, and the other half wanted to scream and walk out. She needed to just think for a moment, to just be away from him. Her emotions were churning inside of her. She understood what Pastor was saying but she felt a sense of dread and agony. He was talking crazy and she did not want to give him any indication that she was accepting the words coming out of his mouth. He was married to Rose, the one person she had grown close to. No matter what her decision she knew that this situation could not possibly end well for everyone involved.

Looking up at Pastor, and knowing that he had raped her, she still felt drawn to him. He was God's man, always in control, always speaking with such authority. She understood that she could not raise the baby alone and getting an abortion was not the answer. It was her baby. She thought about just asking him for money or helping her to place the baby up for adoption, maybe an abortion was the only answer. She decided that it was better to walk in her shame of having a child out of marriage than to carry the sting and guilt of murder.

Pastor interrupted her thoughts and said, "The food will be here soon Sara. Let's have an enjoyable meal. What do you say? Will you trust me?" Looking up at him she nodded yes.

"I need to go to the bathroom," she stated.

Smiling and licking his lips he replied, "Okay, it is in the back on the other side of the bar." He pointed in the direction of the bathroom. She followed his finger and stood up. He took her hand and said, "We will discuss the details when you come back." She smiled and walked towards the bathroom.

On her way she passed the woman still sitting alone at the bar. They made eye contact and again the woman smiled. Returning the smile, she walked past her noticing that the big guy was no longer there. He was a little intimidating and she felt relieved to not have to interact with him. Entering the bathroom, she began to relax. It was dingy and dirty. There were a couple of stalls and one sink with a roll of paper towel sitting on a small metal shelf above it. Realizing that she had left her purse in the booth, she decided that she would splash water on her face and head back. She decided to tell the pastor that she was ready to go and needed to be home before her mother arrived. Turning on the water, she cupped two handfuls of water and gently splashed her face. She reached for the roll of paper towel and quickly tore off a piece and held it to her face. Hearing the door opening she lowered the towel to see the large man who had been standing at the back of the bar talking to the bartender.

"Hey! Hey!" she yelled at him, "This is the girl's bathroom!"

The man, not uttering a word slapped her. For a second, she could only see a shadow where he stood, and she fell to the floor. The shadow grew bigger and was now leaning over her. Sara grabbed his pant leg and tried to pull herself up when he hit her again. This time it was a punch, on the side of her head, just over her left ear. Powerless she tried to raise her head and scream for help when everything faded to black.

A throbbing ache and flashes of sharp pain forced Sara into consciousness. Opening her eyes, she saw a black canvas before her. Her throat was dry, and she could not close her mouth. At first the object in her mouth felt like paper but as it started to melt, she realized that the man had stuffed her mouth full of toilet paper. Fearing she

SPIRITUAL WICKEDNESS IN HIGH PLACES

would choke she resisted the urge to scream. With each passing second, the canvas grew lighter, transitioning to a dark gray. Straining to see through the covering over her head only made her headache worse and only revealed a blurry mass moving about. Thick, rough and meaty hands grabbed at her searching for the best way to maneuver a limp and unresponsive body. The big man fumbled around, cursing in frustration, he latched onto her right arm and leg, jerking her off the floor and effortlessly tossing her over his shoulder. With every step he took, the pain in her head got worse. She felt the sway of his motion as he moved forward. Feeling a breeze across her legs and hearing the crunch of the gravel, she knew that she was no longer in the building. Sara started twisting her body hoping to wiggle free. The man responded by punching her in the side, knocking the wind out of her and submission in. She gasped and started to cry and choke on the dissolving paper. The faint ringing in her ears prevented her from understanding the muffled voices and murmuring in the background however the sound of metal scratching against metal was unmistakable, she knew a door was opening. The voices grew closer and a woman gave orders to others. She yelled for the man carrying Sara to stop moving and walked over in front of him. He abruptly stopped and shifted Sara's weight on his shoulder bringing her body closer to the curve of his neck. The woman reached out and cupped Sara's chin in the palm of her hand, then slowly began lifting the covering over her head, stopping at her mouth.

She yelled at the man holding her, "Are you crazy?" and yanked the toilet paper out of Sara's mouth using her fingers to sweep her throat, causing her to gag.

"You fool, she'll choke to death. You are so f'ing stupid! Do you realize that you're messing with JJ's money? You idiot, ugh!"

She continued to raise the covering. Sara took in a deep breath and tried to form words with her lips, but nothing would come. Her mouth wouldn't move and even the slightest of sounds remained trapped in her throat. She stared at the woman, her eyes filled with shear panic and fear, pleading for help. The woman was the lady in the bar. She grabbed Sara's face, turned it from side to side examining her then abruptly returned the covering to its previous position.

As desperation seeped into Sara's mind, regret took root. She should have listened to her instincts warning her in the car with Pastor Calvin. Something had been telling her she shouldn't go in, but she had gone inside anyway. She felt so stupid. Trusting Pastor Stanfield once had been a mistake. And now doing it again may prove fatal. Where was she going? What was to come?

The man carried Sara to a van parked in the back of the restaurant. The woman from the bar asked him what took so long. Rolling Sara into the van he shrugged and responded, "I had to hit her twice."

The woman shook her head and closed the door. She tapped the driver on the shoulder and said, "Let's roll and get her to the house. We have a three-hour drive and the sooner we get there the better."

The driver responded, "No problem, boss lady."

While the van eased out of the parking lot and onto the street the woman opened a small black leather bag and pulled out a syringe. She grabbed Sara's right arm and tied an eight-inch strip of elastic material around her forearm, tightening it until she could see her veins popping up. While gently inserting the needle into Sara's arm she said, "You are a pretty little thing. One of the pure looking ones. Chris did good, really good with this one."

She injected the morphine into Sara's arm, laid her head on a small pillow, taking care to tilt her head so she would not chock on her own drool, and covered her with a black tarp.

SPIRITUAL WICKEDNESS IN HIGH PLACES

Joey walked up to the booth and set the full order of rib tips in front of Chris. "Mama said to tell you that she has some peach cobbler with your name on it," he said.

"Well, you tell Mama, I said thank you for keeping my food hot. I didn't think the girl would ever go to the bathroom. I thought pregnant women had to pee a lot. As for the cobbler, I honestly can't think of a better way to top off a good evening. And here," sliding an envelope over to Joey, he continued, "Give Mama my tithes for the month," he said winking at Joey and reaching for a rib tip.

Chris noticed that Sara had forgotten her purse. He reached for a wet wipe, cleaned his hands, and picked it up. Looking inside he found her cell phone and the pregnancy test. The phone's message indicator light was on, a smile eased across his face as he listened to a call from her mother, "Sara, I know you wanted to talk tonight, but I am tired and heading to bed. Let's talk over coffee in the morning. I love you. Be safe."

Chris reflected on his favor from God. "Just in time," he thought, pleased that he had acted before things got out of hand. He pulled the sim card out of the phone, laid it on the floor and stomped on it. He dropped the sim card into Sara's ginger ale, finished his meal and walked out the back door.

Calvin watched as the crew drove off with Sara. An hour later Chris emerged with a toothpick in his mouth and wiping his hands. He tossed something in the dumpster and signaled to Calvin to pull up. Calvin asked how everything went.

Looking straight ahead Chris smiled and stated, "Once again, brother, God has shown favor towards us. Take me to see JJ, he will be pleased with how we handled this on our own. Now that he leads the Brotherhood, he stays on our asses about eliminating risk."

Missing

Jen woke up earlier than normal. She was exhausted the night before and passed out after sending Sara a text message. She did not sleep well, tossing and turning through most of the night. It was always difficult to rest when all of her children were not in the house by midnight. Last night two were not home when she went to bed. Greg Jr. and Sara were missing in action. Glancing at her phone she noticed that Sara had not responded to her text message. Jen grabbed her robe and headed down the hall to do a headcount. He was sleeping, still fully dressed and wearing his shoes. He had obviously been up to no good all night. *Probably with that new girlfriend of his,* she thought. She opened the door to Sara's room and immediately noticed that her bed had not been slept in. Running downstairs to check the kitchen and hoping that her daughter would be there waiting for her with a cup of coffee, a sense of dread started to take hold. Her head was telling her to calm down and don't overreact, but her heart was telling her that Sara was in trouble. Her daughter always responded to her text messages.

Entering the kitchen, Jen's hopes were crushed. Everything was as she had left it the night before, including the absence of her daughter. She stood still and straight in the center of the kitchen, her eyes slowly scanning over every square inch, as if Sara could be hiding in plain sight or was too tiny to notice at first glance. The ticks of the clock boomed in her head, slower than the cadence of her heartbeat but just as strong in its pounding.

Pulling at each strand of hope she held onto, she noticed in the corner of her eye, the coffee pot. Jen quickly went over to it and wrapped her hands around it, checking for any remnant of heat. Maybe Sara just got up early to go do something. She had enough chores that Jen wouldn't put an early start past her. Jen had only one strand left as she found the coffee cold and a day old.

Returning to the kids' bedrooms, waking each one to see if they had talked to their sister, her last thread of hope severed as each one told their mother they had not heard from her and had seen her leave. Sara had never spent one night away from home. The constant protective worrying only known to mothers was, in that moment, materializing. Sara had insisted that they needed to talk. However, believing that her daughter wanted to talk about going away to college, she had delayed speaking with her. She was not ready to think about one of her children not being with her, especially Sara who had been her helper since her divorce. At the age of ten, she had taken on grown up responsibilities and was more of a mother than a big sister to her siblings. Working two jobs just to be able to manage basic expenses had left Jen with little time to raise children. When her husband left, she promised her children that they would not move into government housing or apply for food stamps. She committed that nothing would change. Jen put her hopes and dreams aside and at times suffering unbearable stress, she kept fighting to provide for her family. That decision had come with a price. She could not afford to be warm and fuzzy. To keep the kids in line she had to be strict and stern and her tools was discipline and fear. As each year passed, she noted that none of her children used drugs, had ever been arrested, and had not gotten pregnant or impregnated anyone else. So, for her, it was working. But today was different, it felt off and wrong. For the first time in nine years, she was terrified.

I haven't lost a child yet and I'm not going to lose my Sara, she thought as she rushed out of the house, still in her robe and ran across the street to her neighbor Carl's house. He was a police officer and would help. She began beating on his door and ringing the doorbell. Carl opened the door in uniform with his hand on his gun.

"Jen, what the hell is going on?" he asked.

"It's Sara, she did not come home last night. Something is really wrong. Carl, I feel it. Something is very wrong!" she stated, her voice raspy and tight.

Carl started to tell Jen that she needed to wait seventy-two hours before reporting a person missing but looking at her and how distraught she was and knowing she was not someone prone to hysterics, he decided against it. He also knew Sara. She was a good girl and had been active in the local church. He would often see her headed that way with her little brothers and sisters behind her. She looked like a mother hen with her baby chicks tagging along in a single file. "Okay, Jen, go home and get dressed. I will be right over to talk to you," he said.

At that moment Jen realized that she was still in her pajamas and robe. She looked down and grabbed her collar, closing the opening revealing her chest. Tears flowing, she quietly said, "Please hurry, I…I…don't know what to do." Jen turned, walked home and got dressed. While putting on her shoes, she heard a knock at the door. Everyone in the house was awake and questions were flying. "What is going on? Where is Sara? Mom, why are you crying? Is Sara hurt?" the kids asked. Jen told them to be quiet. They continued with the questions, following her down the stairs and to the front door. She opened the door and let Carl inside. He sat them all down in the living room and asked each one when they last saw Sara.

Greg Jr. spoke up first. "She made dinner for us. She didn't eat with us because she was going out to run errands and needed to get ready. I gave her a hard time because she didn't toast my bread. She laughed at me and said that I was making her late." He lowered his head to keep others from seeing his tears.

"Did she say where she was going or what errands?"

Greg Jr. shook his head no. Carl asked the others, but no one had anything more to add. Carl turned to Jen and asked to see Sara's bedroom. Walking into the room, he immediately noticed that her bed was made and what appeared to be two changes of clothing were lying on the bed. It appeared that whatever she was doing she was trying to decide what to wear. Nothing else seemed out of place. He asked Jen if any of her clothes were missing, and she said no. Her brush and comb were still in the bathroom as well as her toothbrush. Carl clicked the button on his walkie-talkie and asked for a detective unit.

For the next six months, Jen and the police department looked for Sara. They discovered that the last ping to her cell phone came from an area in South Bend, Indiana. Detectives visited every business within a two-mile radius. No one had seen her. Flyers with her picture were posted everywhere. The Church, led by Pastor Stanfield, held nightly vigils and organized volunteers to go door to door. The local news channels ran announcements asking if anyone had seen Sara or had information to please call the police. Jen was relentless. She reconciled with her ex-husband as losing her daughter put life in a different light and she came to realize that she needed help, and most of all she needed her husband. Together they were relentless in their pursuit to find their daughter. Rumors started flying that Sara had been abducted, murdered, or had simply grown tired of taking care of her siblings and ran away. As the days grew into years, Jen became grayer and gentler. She never gave up hope and through her loss she learned how to love. She continued to put up flyers and look for her daughter.

Jen

No one is born being hard. Hardness comes on the back of experiences. Each hurt and disappointment leaves behind bits and pieces of itself. Some allow the residue to weaken them and turn them into victims, others allow it to hone them into fighters. Jen allowed her fears, hurt and disappointments to make her tough. Her toughness sharpened her intellect and turned her into a fierce protector.

Life had been good for Jen Robinson. She was beautiful and smart. She had her mother's wit and her daddy's strength. Most of all she had big plans for her life. She would graduate from high school, go to college and get a fancy job in the city away from the sleepy backwards town she grew up in. Everyone that knew her, understood that whatever she set her mind to do she would accomplish it. Some called her competitive, Jen just knew that she was better and wanted to make sure everyone saw it. Her mother was keenly aware that her daughter had surpassed her in many ways and due to her own youth, a part of her was a little jealous. Her dad watched her grow strong and confident and knew that his daughter was going to be somebody important. In his own way he encouraged her. A slight smile, a wink or the tilt of his head let her know that he was watching her and approved, even though he would not outwardly say it.

STEPH BYERS

The competitive streak that kept her at the top of her class also drove her to extremes. What started out as a fun night of roller-skating in early spring, quickly turned into a competition for the attention of a boy. Anna Mae Dempsey was her name. She flaunted around the rink like she owned the placed. She was a tall skinny dark girl. Curls pressed into her head, shiny and crispy looking, she walked around with her nose in the air as if she had caught wind of a cow patty. Jen noticed that she was flirting with Greg Brown. A track star from Central high school in South Bend, Indiana. He was three years older than Jen, kind of cute but more important he was a track star, a lettered athlete and the girls were making a fuss over him. The rink was the hottest spot in town. It was the place where kids were out from under the watchful eye of their parents. The smell of leather and sweaty bodies penetrated the air as the music thumped and mirrored balls spun shards of multicolored lights across the room.

Jen and her friends were leaning over the railing as Greg skated past. He was good, really good. Laughing, she noted how far he swung his right leg out and turning to her friends stated, "He's cute and all but he's gonna kill somebody with that leg!" The others burst into laughter. He smiled and winked at her as he sped by, locked arm in arm with Anna Mae. This boy has the nerve to dare me, Jen thought. "Take note ladies", she said, gliding onto the rink, spinning and dipping to the beat of the music. Just walking into the building, she had the interest of all of the boys. Long wavy hair falling gracefully down her back, full lips, smooth copper skin and a tiny waist that flowed into curvy hips. It was impossible to ignore her presence. As she skillfully owned the floor the boys interest quickly gave way to having their full attention. And Greg took note, and so did Anna Mae. For Jen, she had no real interest in Greg, she just wanted to put Anna Mae in her place. And she would not stop until her mission was accomplished.

SPIRITUAL WICKEDNESS IN HIGH PLACES

As the night of teasing and flirting came to an end, Jen noticed Anna Mae headed for Greg's car. Running over to the car, she hopped into the back seat as Anna Mae eased into the front.

"Why are you here?" Anna Mae asked. She was talking to Jen but looking at Greg. She needed him to put Jen out of the car. If he really liked her, he needed to handle this.

"I'm riding with y'all, right Greg?" she responded. Greg was looking at her through the rearview mirror. He shrugged his shoulders, never taking his eyes off of Jen. Anna Mae witnessed the silent communication between the two of them. Opening the car door, she stepped out and told both to go to hell before slamming it closed and walking away. Having second thoughts and determined to put Jen in her placed, she turned back, hands clenched into tight fists, as Jen jumped into the front seat laughing and Greg pulled away.

Eight months later, Jen was standing next to her mother washing dishes. The kitchen was narrow with just enough room for two people to comfortably move around. She had on a baggy sweatshirt and jeans. It had become her uniform of choice for the past two months, hiding her secret. A secret she had kept from her parents, her school and most of all Greg. Her pregnancy. Time was getting away from her. Every day she mulled over her perceived options, considering the pros and cons of each; give the baby away, let Greg have it, run away and just take care of it herself. All the desperate imaginations of a 17-year-old child having to make adult decisions.

As her mother brushed past her and touched the bump that was housing her developing grandchild, any plans she had quickly dissipated from the ensuing chaos. An emotional overreacting whirlwind ensued and before the week was out a plan had been solidified by her parents. She was not given a choice, her mother had insisted and her father, the one who knew her best, allow her mother to chart the path. Within three weeks, without having a voice she became hostage to tradition and was forced to marry a boy she did not love. No one consulted her about her dreams, nor did they sit and reason with her about options. For the first time in her life, she felt the sting of abandonment.

As time went by abandonment was joined by betrayal as she tried to make the best of a life that was not meant to be her life. It all felt surreal, even as her other children were born, she struggled to hold onto the hope of having something close to the life she imaged for herself and the tug of motherhood. Two people forced to marry never commit to each other. They either commit to their situation or the struggle to survive it. Jen and Greg struggled to survive it. Their marriage had its highpoints however the lows brought about by affairs, financial struggles and small-town interferences took their toll. Deciding that if she was going to survive with at least a piece of herself in tack, she had to correct her biggest mistake; she divorced Greg.

Having looked at all of the angles and anticipating all of the difficulties, she was ready to move forward. Every dream she had would be realized through her children. She would make them strong and independent; failure was not an option. Her children would not have to beg, they would not be weak nor experience defeat. The reigns she placed on each child tightened as they grew older. The strictness of her rules hid the fear of failure, the sharpness of her tongue covered the hint of weakness and the quickness of her hand masked the undying love and desire to make them strong. She committed to sending forth into a world that had betrayed her four kings and two queens.

Forsaken

Sara woke up with a splitting headache. It hurt to move her head from side to side. When she tried to sit up, she felt a sharp pain on the left side of her face. She could not lift her arms and realized that her hands and her feet were strapped down to a hospital bed. She felt something strange and bulky between her legs. It felt like a thick sanitary napkin. Her throat was sore and hurt so bad that she could not yell or speak above a whisper. As her eyes adjusted to the lighting, she looked around the room. There was a folding chair in the corner next to a small table with a lamp on it. She saw a twin sized bed on the opposite side of the room. Next to the hospital bed she was in was a pole with a bag of clear liquid in it. A tube ran from the bag to her arm. She could not figure out what happened to her. She remembered having dinner with the Pastor and going into the bathroom, but she could not remember anything else.

There was too much happening for her to register it all. But one thing she did know was that she wasn't meant to be here and that something was wrong. Sara started to cry, silent choking sobs as she struggled to breathe through all the emotion and turmoil.

She heard the door rattling and creaking as it opened. A woman walked over to her. "I see you are awake. Thank goodness. We thought you were going to die. I'm Cassie, your handler. You and I are going to be particularly good friends, sugar," she said.

Cassie was a masculine woman. She had a stocky build and was quite handsome. With the neatly trimmed faded hair cut one could easily cause someone to mistake her for a man from behind. The tone of her voice was smooth and easy, and she spoke in a no-nonsense way, short and curt.

Sara recognized the woman from the bar and asked "Where am I and what happened to me? I'm pregnant, please help me, you have to help me" she begged.

Cassie looked at Sara and almost felt sorry for her. She began taking the IV out of her arm. This was her eighth girl. She had a good track record of breaking them in fast. First, she took away all of their hope, then, if needed she would beat the fight out of them and start replacing who they thought they were with who she needed them to be. The younger ones were easier. This girl was different, and she had thought Chris was making a mistake in claiming her. But when she saw her walk into the diner, everything became clear. She had this purity about her, a simple elegant beauty. Every man that wanted to have sex with their daughters, their kids friends, the Bible schoolteacher, or the choir girl would enjoy having a piece of her. She figured they had at least four good years before she would lose everything that made her special. When that time came, they would move her to the block in Las Vegas. For now, private auditions in New York would do. But first she had to be molded.

Cassie cleaned Sara up and changed the pad between her legs. Turning to walk out of the door she looked back at Sara and said, "Let's get one thing clear. I am here to help you. I will teach you to do your job. If you do it well, your life will be extremely easy. I've learned that sweet little things like you end up enjoying the life more than others. So, the sooner you get with the program, the better. And don't worry, you are no longer pregnant. Chris left specific instructions to end the pregnancy."

As the door closed you could hear Sara begin to wail. She sounded like a wounded animal. The burning in her throat worsened but she continued, she needed the pain. She cried out to God, "What did I do, please tell me what I did to cause you to hate me? Oh God, oh my God," she sobbed, "please forgive me, please."

In shock she cried herself to sleep. She dreamed of being chased by dogs. They were Dobermans. They chased her into an abandoned house and cornered her in a room, biting and growling, ripping at her clothes. One lunged at her and caught the front of her blouse, shredding it and exposing her breast. She covered herself with her arms and closed her eyes as she waited on the pain of their teeth sinking into her skin. All at once they stopped and the room was silent. She felt them licking her. Sara opened her eyes and saw a man touching her breast. His hands were wet.

"Stop!" she yelled.

"Oh, hello dear. You had everyone worried. You have been asleep for three days. I am Doctor Ronnie. Cassie called me, worried that she may have given you too much morphine," he said.

Doctor Ronnie was big, dark and shiny black. He was tall and had a fat belly. His hands were clammy and unusually big, she thought. He wore wire rimmed glasses that rested at the end of his nose and he was looking at her as if she were something to eat. He continued to touch her.

She yelled at him to stop. "If you are a doctor, please help me." she said. "These people have taken me, and they killed my baby. My name is Sara, my mom's name is Jen Robinson. I am from Elkhart, Indiana. Please help me," she begged.

"Oh, I don't need to know all that girl. I am here only to check you out and make sure that you are okay. And you are. Your body has healed nicely," he said.

He pulled the sheet off of her, exposing her naked body. He lifted each of her legs and placed them into the stirrups and strapped them down. She felt the bed fold away underneath her and realized that he was about to give her a pelvic exam. Instead, he unbuckled his pants. Determined to fight, Sara tried to kick him, twisting her body away from him and screaming. He stood between her legs and slapped her. And he raped her. It seemed like it took forever but it only lasted a few minutes. He collapsed on top of her gasping for air. She closed her eyes, refusing to look at him. The stench of his oily musky body filled her nostrils causing her retch. He stood up, pinched her thigh and pulled up his pants. He never took his eyes off of her as he smiled and ran his tongue over his teeth. He banged on the door and Cassie came into the room.

"How is she doc?" she asked.

"She is good to go. Everything, and I mean everything is working just fine," he said.

"Well, that will be $250," Cassie stated as she held out her hand.

"What do you mean, $250?" he asked.

"I told you that I would examine her in exchange for a play," he stated.

"Yeah, Doc, but you slapped her. I was watching. And yo ass is nasty. When is the last time you took a bath? For real, man, you are a doctor. Give me the money or I will need to talk to JJ," she stated half laughing and half repulsed.

Doctor Ronnie handed over the $250 dollars and made Cassie promise that she would not tell JJ. Cassie waited until Ronnie left the

SPIRITUAL WICKEDNESS IN HIGH PLACES

room. She turned to Sara. Her face was red but not bruised so she put the money in her pocket. No need to involve JJ at all.

It had been two weeks since they took Sara. Everyone was looking for her. Cassie overheard Chris and JJ discussing the police showing up at Big Willey's. They showed Joey a picture of her and asked if she had been in the bar. He told them that he had not seen her. The police pressed him further and asked if anything unusual happened lately. He told them nothing out of the ordinary and everything was business as usual. They also asked if there was a security camera on the premises and he told them no there was not.

Cassie knew that after six weeks things would die down and they could move Sara to New York. In the meantime, she might as well make some money and so she scheduled some plays for Sara.

With her hope of ever being found shaken, Sara tried to pray, but it was as if God did not hear her. Each prayer seemed to only result in more strange men raping her. This manifested as anger within her and in return she stopped trying to hear from God. The still small voice was gone. She learned quickly not to fight. Each time she did, Cassie would punish her. She would drug her and make her go days without food. Sara hated being drugged. She could not remember anything. But each time she was out of it, plays kept happening. She would wake up and find herself dressed in costumes: a choir robe, a preacher's collar, a school uniform, and another time she was wearing a baby bib and diaper. She could smell the stench of the men who raped her. She worried about getting pregnant. She worried about losing her soul. Her mother had told her how important it was to not lie down with just any man. To save herself for someone who deserved and loved her. She said to her, "No matter what any man says to you, remember that you are special. Every time a man ejaculates inside of you, he leaves a part of who he is and takes away a part of who you are. That kind of gift only belongs to the person that God has chosen for you."

STEPH BYERS

Sara cried and longed for her mother, the wisdom, the strength and yes, even the discipline. She understood now that her mother was protecting her and teaching her how to be strong. Drawing from her mother's strength, Sara stopped fighting. She started looking for a way out.

New York City

Cassie noticed the difference in Sara. She had stopped fighting and seemed resigned to her new life. It is always a good sign when the girls stop praying, asking for their mamas, and calling out to God. Sara however stopped talking altogether. When anyone spoke to her, she responded with one word or a shrug. This made Cassie very suspicious and she decided it was time to move her to the Agency and advise Miss Ivy to not send her out for private auditions or parties but to only work her inside.

The Towers Classic Modeling Agency on Fifth Avenue in New York would be the perfect place to send her. Most of the girls there were younger than Sara and came from all over the world.

The building was twenty-five stories high. The first through the tenth floors were offices, the eleventh through the fifteenth floors was home to the agency and the 16th through the 25th floors were private high-end apartments. The agency had private lounges on each floor. Most of the new girls were told that they were just there to be nice to wealthy men and party. All were eager to do this thinking that the men would hire them as models or even marry them. Many came from other countries and spoke little or no English at all. Some were as young as fifteen. The private parties were called auditions. Each girl was paid to attend the auditions, but they never seemed to make enough money to leave since the Agency charged them for room, meals, medical checkups and helping them obtain work visas. Every girl was charged for everything, including a bar of soap to keep them in debt. The agency controlled their every move, not allowing the girls to go out alone, watch tv or make phone calls. They were trapped.

Miss Ivy, the head talent scout, loved Sara's look. Although her eyes were lifeless, there was a pure innocence that emanated from her. She was a special girl, and Ivy referred to her as the "Special One." Sara endured another five years of being raped. Most of her auditions resulted in complaints. She had mastered the art of lifelessness, often staring at her defilers, making them uncomfortable or forcing the realization that just maybe they were doing something very wrong. Although many of them offered numerous complaints, none of the men turned her away and they all paid up in the end. Miss Ivy said that was all that mattered.

Sara found New York City to be a lonely place, even though she shared a bedroom with five other girls. None of them attempted to get to know each other. Anyone caught becoming too friendly would be punished or removed from the Agency. Confined to the building she could only look out the window at all of the people passing by. She often imagined where they were going and what they were doing. She wondered if any of those people could be one of her sisters or brothers and if they could feel her presence or sense something strange as they walked by the building. But no one ever looked up.

For years, Sara endured the isolation. Some of the men who raped her worked for the government. She thought they were not as bad as some of the others. Most were insecure and only talked about themselves. The wealthy men were cruel and sadistic. They saw all of the girls as disposable meat. It was not the best life, but it was the life that she had become accustomed to living. She had given up on finding a way out. It had become impossible.

On a day like any other, the rain poured down on the streets of New York. The sun was hidden by the sad and gloomy clouds. Lightening flashed periodically across the sky without its usual partner, thunder. Umbrellas peppered the street and people rushed in a hurry to get out of the rain. Sara watched them and wished that she could be hidden by one of the big umbrellas. Startled by a hand on her shoulder, Sara instinctually pulled away and turned around to find Miss Ivy standing behind her. Deep in thought, Sara had not heard her approaching. "Sorry, Miss Ivy. I hadn't heard you," Sara answered, turning fully toward the woman.

"Well, I have a surprise for you. Have you been on an airplane before?"

Shaking her head, Sara said, "No, ma'am."

"Well, today is your lucky day. You are going to Las Vegas, Nevada to work the strip. You will be able to go outside and there will be other girls around that are more like you," she said.

"Why?" Sara asked. "I don't cause any trouble. I keep to myself, so why do I have to go?"

Miss Ivy shook her head "Special girl, you just don't get it, do you? It is time to go, honey. You ain't so special anymore. JJ said to move you out."

"But why?" Sara asked again.

"Because fresh ass is coming in, we need to make room. You have gotten too old for auditions with our clientele. Now, Cassie is going to go with you. Listen and do exactly what she tells you to do. Understood?" Miss Ivy asked.

Sara nodded and returned to looking out the window until the night sky was illuminated by city lights. She wondered if Las Vegas would be the place she would die, after all she was no longer special.

It was 10:00 pm when Cassie showed up. She brought a pair of jeans, white t-shirt, tennis shoes and a black hooded sweatshirt. She told Sara to get dressed. She handed her a pair of black rimmed glasses and told her to put those on as well. Cassie watched her get dressed and as soon as she was finished, she grabbed her by the arm and led her out of the building. There were a lot of people on the street, but no one even glanced in their direction. They walked about a block and got into a black cargo van. It had a pillow and a black tarp in the back. Cassie told her to sit on the tarp and directed the driver to head to the airport.

"We are flying Delta," she said.

The driver responded, "Yes, boss lady. When will you be back?"

"Soon," she responded.

The ride to the airport was eerily quiet. Sara wondered if this was what happened to the other girls. The van stopped in front of the airport. Cassie got out and opened the side door. She held her hand out and Sara reluctantly took it and was unexpectantly jerked out of the van. Stumbling to the ground she looked up and saw the scowl on Cassie's face. She understood the reminder of who was in charge.

"Listen, no trouble. Don't make eye contact with anyone, do not speak to anyone, head down and do what you are told. You got it?" Cassie said. As they approached the doors, Cassie grabbed Sara's arm, squeezing it as she brought Sara's ear close to her lips. "I asked if you got it."

"Yes," Sara responded.

SPIRITUAL WICKEDNESS IN HIGH PLACES

Walking through the airport, it was as if they were invisible. No one looked their way or stopped to ask why they did not have any luggage. Sara had never been in an airport. People were everywhere. She smelled food cooking, heard kids crying and someone making announcements through the speaker every two minutes. Walking through security she kept her head down and would not respond to anyone. When the TSA agent asked for her ID and boarding pass, she looked at Cassie who smiled and said, "I have it. Here it is, sir." The agent thought it was strange that an adult was not speaking for herself but looking at the massive number of people in line, he shrugged it off, scanned the ID and initialed her boarding pass waving them through. He deliberately handed Sara her boarding pass and said, "You have a good day, Trina." Sara looked at him and then glanced down at her ID. It had her picture on it and the name Trina Bouche. She started to ask Cassie about it, but before she could say anything, Cassie snatched the ID out of her hand and hissed, "What did I tell you?" Sara lowered her head and followed her through the security checkpoint.

Cassie and Sara arrived at the gate just in time to board. They sat in first class. The flight attendant noticed that Sara would not look up and thought that it was very strange. Whenever she asked the younger woman if she wanted anything to eat or drink, she would look at the older woman and let her respond. Having recently completed sex trafficking training and learning how to spot a victim, the attendant was not sure if this was it. She only knew that something was not right. She could not get this wrong and risk someone complaining to the airlines. That could cause her to lose her job.

Halfway through the flight, she noticed the younger woman standing up. The woman with her had fallen asleep and was startled by the younger woman's movement. She grabbed her by the arm, and they started to talk. Thinking that the young woman might be headed to the bathroom, she decided to take advantage of the opportunity to ask her if she needed help.

The flight attendant wrote a note on a napkin and pulled out a card with a helpline number on it and quickly placed it in the bathroom. She emptied the bathroom trash in case the older woman was watching her and was suspicious.

As Sara approached the front of the plane, she reached for the handle to the wrong bathroom. Stopping her, the attendant pointed to the other one and entered the restroom to remove the trash. As she glanced into the first-class cabin, she noticed the older woman watching her.

Sara entered the restroom. It was so small, she thought. Cassie told her she had three minutes to go and return to her seat. Looking at the toilet she wondered if flushing it sent everything out into the air. Shrugging, she used it and flushed. She noticed a napkin and a card next to the sink. Someone had written on the napkin, "If you are being held against your will, if someone is forcing you to have sex, if you need help, please look at me when I come to your seat." Sara picked up the card. It had a helpline number on it. It said *Stop Sex Trafficking* in bold red letters. Sara put the card in her underwear and placed the note in the toilet and flushed it. She knew that if Cassie found it, she would be beaten and drugged. Leaving the bathroom, she kept her head down and resisted the urge to look for the attendant. Returning to her seat, Cassie grabbed her arm digging her fingernails into her skin. She said, "You took four minutes." Within a minute of sitting down, the attendant approached them and asked if they would like something to drink and held out a basket of snacks. Sara pulled the hood over her head and looked out the window.

Sara knew that the card and the note were not the way to escape anything. She also knew that Cassie would hurt this woman and not

SPIRITUAL WICKEDNESS IN HIGH PLACES

give it a second thought. The flicker of hope rising in her stomach quickly passed as Sara realized that she could not put the flight attendant in danger. Having felt the pain of Cassie's wrath and remembering the stern warning accompanied by the bruises on her arm, she knew that she would not say a word... She stayed still in her seat and never made eye contact.

The flight attendant never returned to their seats. Upon landing she watched the two women walk up the causeway and prayed that she had done the right thing, hoping that things were not as they seemed.

Trina

It was dark when they arrived in Las Vegas. There were signs and lights everywhere. From neon signs to streetlamps, it was all nearly blinding, instilling awe and a hint of fear in Sara's eyes and heart. Her life had taught her that the unknown always resulted in pain. After getting into a taxi, Cassie told the driver to take them to a place called the Pink Lady Ranch, which was just off of the strip. About twenty minutes later, the car was pulling into the gates of a sprawling ranch with grass that glowed green from the lights that lined the driveway and paved the way to a canopied area where they came to a stop. Sara saw a few other buildings that all seemed to connect to the one they were in front of. Each of those buildings, she counted five of them, had dim lights speckled throughout. As they stepped out of the car, a tall muscular man with red hair emerged from the darkness. Had he been waiting on them?

The man was smiling and waved at them. "Hey, Cassie. How long will you be with us this time?" He was talking and moving, never stopping long enough to make eye contact with either one. He brushed past them and closed the taxi door, nodding at the driver and hitting the roof twice to signal him to take off. He grabbed Sara's ass and gave it a firm pinch.

Cassie replied, "I'm only here long enough to close this deal then I'm out."

"Well, let's get it done," he answered, leading them into the building.

SPIRITUAL WICKEDNESS IN HIGH PLACES

Sara quickened her pace to keep up with the two. Not sure of what to expect next she needed to stay as close to Cassie as possible. However dangerous, Cassie was the only familiar thing she had, and she figured she'd end up in the least amount of trouble by staying close.

They passed by a lounge with circular leather chairs and tables. Next to the lounge was a bar. Glass double doors were propped open and Sara could see half naked women leaning over men, sitting on their laps, and dancing to intoxicating music. They were oblivious to being watched and not one of them looked her way.

Their escort stopped them in their tracks with a signal, he raised his hand, palm facing outwards, then one finger in the air. He stepped inside the doorway of the lounge and placed his thumb and index finger in his mouth and whistled. The loud and piercing sound demanded everyone's attention. The music halted and he called out, "Candy, come here."

A black girl emerged. She was very thin, and her skin was the color of coffee with a lot of cream. She wore a blonde wig that went down to her waist, and her thickly applied eye shadow was a bright blue. The color drew attention to her left eye that wandered in any given direction.

"Take Trina to her room," the man ordered. He then turned to Sara. "Go with her."

Sara did not talk to the girl. Instead, like a robot, she disconnected and did as she was told.

The girl tried to engage Sara in conversation, electing to walk only a step-in front of her so that they were almost side by side. "Hey, I'm Candy Cane. You can call me CC like everyone else. I have been here for seven years now. How long you been dating?"

Sara looked at her, puzzled.

"You know, turning tricks, selling yo ass, you know, girl," Candy said stopping in front of a door with the room number one eleven. " Here we go, this is your new home."

Sara turned away and did not respond. The room was clean, and her bed was bigger than what she had before. To the left there was a closet with clothes in it. She saw dresses, lingerie short skirts, and blouses that looked more like bras, and gowns hanging to the left. Beneath the clothes were shoes neatly lined in order of heal height, four inches to kitten healed slippers.

"There're more clothes in the dresser over there," she told Sara, pointing to the corner. After a few seconds of swiftly flipping through several gowns hanging in the closet, CC pulled out a blue sheer gown with tulle trim and covered in sequins. "Put this on Trina." And after a moment, she added, "Nothing underneath."

Sara turned her back to CC and unzipped her pants. Remembering the card that she got on the airplane she cupped it and folded it into her clothes and placed them on the bed. CC noticed the purple and blue discoloration on Sara's back. This made her incredibly sad and she vowed to become her friend and look out for her. Sara slid into the gown. When she was done, CC opened the door to the room and motioned for her to follow.

Approaching the front of the building, Sara could see the tall man that had met them at the car still talking with Cassie. Across from the glass doors leading into the bar stood two wooden doors from the floor to the ceiling. The weight of the doors caused the men to lean back as they pulled them open. CC and Sara were escorted into a dimly lit office. The office was dimly lit. The walls were paneled, and a large desk sat in the middle of the room. To the right of the desk was a big candle. The candlestick was waist high, about three feet. The candle that sat on top of it was so large that a person would have to use two

SPIRITUAL WICKEDNESS IN HIGH PLACES

hands to lift it. The flames dancing from four wicks cast shadows on the wall. To the left of the desk was a leather couch and two leather chairs. Two men in black pants and black t-shirts stood on either side of the door. A short, fat, red-faced white man sat behind the desk smoking a cigar.

Sara could not help but notice how short and stubby his fingers were. He had rings on each of his fingers. His bald head drew attention to the scab on his forehead above his left eye.

The fat man pointed at Cassie and asked, "What do yawl have for me this time, Miss Cassie?" He spoke with a thick southern accent.

Referring to him only as Sir, Cassie stepped forward and said, "Sir, I have a pretty little thing from the Midwest. She used to look pure, but some of that shine is off her now. She does as she is told, and that back ain't broke yet. It is bent but not broke. JJ wants to do business. He says that there is another 10 to 15 years on her."

"What he want fah her?" Sir asked.

"20 Gs," Cassie responded.

Sir motioned for Sara to move forward. Frozen with fear, Sara tried to step forward but could not move. The tall man, with the red hair, stepped behind her and nudged her forward. As she moved toward the desk, Cassie reached over and unhooked her gown causing it to fall to the floor. Humiliated, Sara stood naked staring at her feet. Sir stood up and walked around the desk. He placed his mouth on her breast and inserted a stubby finger inside of her. She tried to step away but the tall man behind her pushed her forward.

Sir licked his finger and said, "I will give you 15. She is pretty all right, but the gal ain't fully broke yet. You Yankees don't know how to break-em right. Must be them little dicks they got."

He started laughing and the other men in the room laughed with him. Cassie agreed on the fifteen thousand dollars. JJ only wanted ten and would be happy that she was able to negotiate an extra five grand. That would score big points with him. She put a hand on Sara's shoulder and said, "Trina, do good for this man. Sir ain't nobody to play with. You were made for this. Chris knew it when he claimed you." She gave her shoulder an extra pat and walked out of the room.

Standing naked in a room with two men at the door, the tall man now near the candle and Sir in front of her, Sara did not know what to expect. For the first time since her abduction, she wanted to die. The two-men stepped forward and grabbed each of her arms. Sir stared at her. His face was so close to hers that she could smell his rancid breath. Suddenly feeling a burning pain on her right shoulder, she started to scream. Sir placed his mouth over hers and as she yelled out in pain, he inhaled her screams. To anyone watching it appeared as if they were embraced in an awkward kiss. The men let her go and she fell to her knees, her mind went blank as she gave into the pain. Sir signaled them to open the doors. CC walked in and seeing Sara struggling to get up she grabbed her by the waist she whispered to her, "C'mon now, don't give up, I got cha, c'mon get up." She pulled Sara's left arm around her shoulder, her gown draped around her, exposing her nakedness, and walked her back to her bedroom. As they passed, the bar men sitting, and drinking raised their glasses to her and let out a few cat calls.

CC helped her put on a night gown and get into bed. She placed a cool cloth on her forehead and bandaged her arm. Adjusting the cloth, she said, "Hey Trina, girl. You have got to get tough. Sir is nasty and all, but he is okay if you don't make him mad. Just stay out of his way and you will be alright. Oh, I got rid of your clothes. No need to invite trouble, you feel me?

Sara looked at the bandage on her shoulder. "What is this?" she asked.

SPIRITUAL WICKEDNESS IN HIGH PLACES

"Oh, so you can talk! That is your mark. We all got them, see mine," CC said, pulling her shirt back to reveal a branded S. "That is to let other pimps and the police know that we belong to Sir."

Sara knew about the police but was not sure how or why she would see pimps. In New York, she auditioned for men from the FBI, CIA, State police as well as governors, mayors, and rich businessmen. She wondered if she would now be forced to have sex with pimps. But just like with the others, she would show her resistance by not moving or making a sound during sex. That was her secret way of not letting them break her.

"Trina, what you thinkin 'bout?" CC asked her. Sara could tell that CC was not very bright. Something about her made Sara realize that she was a victim too. The sad thing was that she did not seem to know it.

Sara looked at her and said, "My name is Sara. What is wrong with your eye?"

CC looked at her and responded "My name is Elizabeth. And Sir is what happened to my eye."

"I'm sorry, Elizabeth," Sara responded.

"Aw, no problem. They said he knocked sense into me, so I guess I ought to be happy 'bout that. I don't know where my sense was, I don't remember much anymore. Except, I like bacon. Sir smells like bacon when he is on me. Now don't you worry about him, his dick is really little and if you stick your finger in his ass he comes in seconds. Not minutes, girl, but seconds," CC giggled.

Sara decided to stop talking. She was not sure what to make of CC or if she could trust her. CC asked her if she wanted to be twins. She told Sara that twins walked the strip together and sometimes if a trick wanted two girls for threesomes they could double up. They also looked out for each other. Sara said yes and CC told her not to worry because she would teach her the rules.

Later that night, Sir came into her room. CC was right, he smelled like bacon. And Sara thought she heard him snort at least twice. He told her that tomorrow she would be on the strip. Her mark for the night was 2,500 dollars and if she did not make her mark, she would be punished.

The entire interaction between the two of them, including the conversation, lasted fifty-nine seconds.

The Strip

The strip was always crowded regardless of the time of day or night. It wasn't actually in Las Vegas but south of the city. Sara came to understand that Sir was her pimp. This was important because lots of girls walked the strip. Each group has a designated area. The pimps claim their blocks and defend them. They also try to lure each other's girls away. The Strip is four miles of hotels, casinos, resorts, restaurants. and girls. A lot of the girls wanted to work for the Pink Lady Ranch. They knew that the ranch was huge. It had forty-two rooms, a nice bar and restaurant, all on one level. Each girl had their own clothes and bedroom. The bedrooms had half baths. There were several shared showers with hot tubs and saunas. Many of the other girls lived in filthy apartments and rat-infested motels.

Sara had been walking it for three weeks now. At first, she could not fathom how she would earn 2,500 a day. Some of the sexual acts she was asked to do were so crazy that she flat out refused. Some men and women offered drugs to her so she would loosen up. There were times when she was tempted to take them, but something inside of her would not let her.

Feeling hopeless, she had nowhere to go, no money and did not know anyone. She no longer had faith or trust. She had even walked away from God. What God would allow her to go through this? For what purpose, for whose benefit? She missed her family but, in her shame, she knew that she could never go home now. The guilt and self-hate dug deeper and deeper into her soul. Each day she could feel what little hope she had held onto dwindle as the callouses hardened on her stiletto tortured feet. Each morning she awoke with dry eyes. Her faith was gone, and she allowed herself to exist in the empirical. Although there wasn't anyone she could trust, CC had grown on her like an annoying little sister. She just had a way of looking on the bright side of everything. Her childlike optimism and simple-minded intellect had grown on her and although it was CC who quietly entered her room to comfort her when she would cry in the middle of the night, she was unable to completely trust her and let her in.

What Sara understood was how to survive, so she kept to herself to stay out of trouble. Determining to live didn't mean, at least in her mind, that she had given in - No, she hadn't. But the light she used to see at the end of her tunnel was smaller than ever, barely even a flicker, about the size of a mustard seed. So, Sara walked the strip for twelve hours a day. After all, she was made for this. And at 2,500 a day, she only had to make 209.00 an hour.

Hope

It was Sunday and business on the strip was slow. Sara had been walking the strip for five years now and nothing surprised her anymore. She noticed a nice-looking mature woman stopping and talking to each girl. She imagined that this is what her mom looked like. The woman was handing flyers to the girls. Some nodded and gave her a hug. Others would throw it in the air, shake their heads and walk away. She approached Sara and said hello. Sara said hi and looked nervously down the street to see if others were watching and wondering if the woman was a cop.

"Baby, my name is Martha. I walk the strip when I can, hoping to help girls in trouble. What's your name, sweetheart?" she said.

Sara felt drawn to the woman but took a step back. Looking away she responded "Trina, I'm Trina."

"Really, I could have sworn the Lord told me that your name was Sara, "she said. Startled, she started to say something but instead closed her mouth and took another step back. The woman took Sara by the hand and placed a flyer in it. She smiled at her and walked away without saying another word.

Sara looked at the flyer. It said, *"When you are tired, when you are ready to go home, when you can't take anymore, wear something red. We can keep you safe, we can get you home. Just wear red."*

Sara looked up and noticed others watching her. She balled up the flyer and threw it. *"Another do-gooder,"* she thought, *"this woman is trying to get me killed. What kind of Vegas trick is this, guessing my name?"*

Later that night at the ranch, Sir sent for her. When she walked into his office, he was sitting on the couch talking to CC. He told her that she and CC were going to work a private party and they were to be on their best behavior. He said that these were extremely important people worth a lot of money, and they had paid a hundred thousand dollars for them so they should make sure that the clients were happy and satisfied. CC was excited and promised Sir that they would make his friends very happy.

Walking back to their rooms, CC told her that Sir wanted them to dress in black lace gowns and to put their hair up. He wanted them to dress exactly alike. Four other girls would be going with them.

Sara found a dress, three-inch stiletto sandals, jewelry, and perfume on her bed. There were rhinestone hair clips next to the shoes. She braided her hair in a single braid and wrapped it into a bun at the base of her skull. As if on cue, each of the girls opened the door to their bedroom and stepped into the hallway. All were dressed identical. Falling in line behind each other they were escorted to a limo with tinted windows. None of the girls spoke. They all wondered what the night would bring. CC grabbed Sara's hand and squeezed it. She leaned over and said "One night at a time. Maybe tonight we will get somethin' special to eat like shrimps." Sara smiled and shook her head. Only CC could think of something positive in the middle of the unknown. Another girl grunted and took some pills.

After a few hours on the road, the limo came to a stop in front of a beautiful oceanside mansion. Sara had never seen a house so big or beautiful. As each girl walked through the front door, they were given a room number and a key. They were instructed to go to their assigned room and take off all of their clothes, leave their heels on, lay on the bed, and wait. Each girl followed a maid down the hall to their rooms. Before entering her room, she made eye contact with CC. Smiling, CC gave her a quick nod and blew her a kiss. *"One night at a time,"* Sara thought and walked through the door.

Sara's room was beautiful. There was a large canopy bed, a separate bathroom, a large sitting area, and a table with food on it. She saw the shrimp on the table and thought of CC and laughed, happy that they had become friends. She walked over to the table and took a few bites of the food. There was a plate of brownies that she could not resist. She quickly ate two of them. Within fifteen mins she started to feel a little dizzy. She took off her clothes and laid naked on the bed. As she was falling asleep, three men walked into her room. Someone yelled at her to get up. She stood beside the bed and a man walked over and hit her. She struggled to maintain her balance, one-foot crossing in front of the other. For the first time in a long time, she let herself get angry.

Letting out a guttural scream she stood and lunged at the man swinging wildly. The others started laughing as Sara was getting the best of him. She scratched him from his ear across his cheek to his chin. He screamed, wiped his face, and looked at the blood on his hand. Grabbing her by the waist he threw her onto the bed. The other two men ran to help hold her down. One grabbed her arms and pulled them over her head. The other grabbed her legs. She kicked him, and the heel of her shoe caught him on his forehead. Angry he punched her in the face. That night the men took turns viciously raping her. At times she lost consciousness and would awaken to them biting her. It seemed as if this would never end. Sara was not aware of when the abuse stopped. She only remembered being in an empty room, bleeding and sore. Two women came in and cleaned her up. They put her dress on and tied her shoes around her waist with a strip of cloth.

Her face was swollen and bruised. She noticed that the women helping her would not make eye contact with anyone. They never spoke to her or each other. It was as if, by not engaging they were not participating, however it was obvious that they had done this often, working in tandem, efficiently going about their business.

The women helped her walk out to the limo, and she noticed other girls being helped. One girl had lashes across her back where she had been whipped, her dress shredded. She looked for CC and didn't see her. A girl draped in a sheet was carried out and placed in the limo. After they were inside, someone knocked three times on the glass and the car drove away. Each girl looked at the other. Some were crying, others were in shock, one girl was nodding and drooling.

Not seeing CC, Sara moved over to the girl wrapped in a sheet and uncovered her. There she was. Her eyes wide open and vacant, she was looking up as if she were searching the heavens. A rope was tied around her neck with pieces of plastic sticking out. There were scratches around her throat as if she had been clawing, trying to grab the rope. Sara kissed her forehead and closed CC's eyes. She placed the sheet back over her face and sat next to her and held her hand during the ride.

As each minute passed, Sara could feel CC's hand growing colder and colder. She held onto it, her grip growing tighter and tighter, she tried to will her back to life as the memories of when they first met flooding her mind provided little comfort. Her mouth struggled to find its place between sorrow and fondness, a smile or a grimace, as she recalled the day CC asked her if she wanted to be twins.

Sara sat in silence during the ride back to the ranch. When the limo finally came to a stop, she raised her friend's hand to her mouth and gently kissed it. The other girls who had been sobbing suddenly became eerily quiet as they left the car one at a time. Staying until she was alone with CC, she couldn't bring herself to leave her. One of the bodyguards yelled at her to get out of the car. Sara raised the sheet one last time and kissed her forehead as she lovingly mouthed a final silent goodbye. She stepped out of the car on her own, refusing to accept a helping hand. Entering the main entrance and walking towards her room she began stripping herself of her tattered clothes and what little feelings she had allowed to creep in and naked walked, numb to her surroundings, down the hall to the bathroom. The hot water stung against her bruised and battered body. She tried to scrub away the pain, both physical and emotional. Her hands ached as she wrapped herself in a towel, the steam rising from her skin. She knew that she was going to be sore the next morning. In some ways she would welcome the soreness, maybe it would distract her from the grief she felt creeping into her heart. She quietly made her way back to her bedroom. Sir appeared in the hallway and congratulated the girls who attended the house of horrors and told them that they had done well. Their reward was a few hours off to rest before heading back to the strip at 10:00 pm. It was 3:00 pm when Sara laid her head on the pillow. Sir watched Sara. He knew how close she and CC had become. He noticed something different in her. He could not tell what it was, just that the timid girl who was known for looking at the floor or away, was now staring him directly in his eyes.

Drifting off to sleep, she allowed herself, for the first time in years to think of her family. She dreamt she was home standing in her kitchen over a sink full of dishes. Her mother was scolding her for not finishing the laundry. Instead of rolling her eyes and silently hating her mother, she apologized and tightly hugged her, nesting her face into her mother's neck and deeply inhaling taking in the scent of her perfume and the warmth of her body. She promised her mother that everything would be done before she got home from work. A single tear rolled down her cheek as she held onto her dream and fought the urge to wake up.

Martha, sat at her kitchen table, praying as her team left the room. Her hands were folded into a fist, and she leaned forward whenever she spoke. Grace was the only word to describe her presence. Her very essence exuded the spirit of peace and forgiveness that had been bestowed upon her by God. All who worked with Martha could sense when she had entered into communion with the holy spirit. Someone without the gift of interpretation heard a foreign language, one that was unknown and hard to describe. To others it was the sweet sound of an easy conversation. The team could hear Martha shout, "Yes, Lord!" three times and after a brief moment of silence they heard her say, "Amen." This was their signal that it was ok to join her at the table.

Moving her gaze from one person to the next as she spoke, "This girl, Sara, is ready. You know how these girls can be timid as deer, but the Lord is showing me something different in her. I… I hadn't even known her name until I saw her face. Just as God revealed her name to me, he has also shown me that she is ready. The time of her healing has come, and we must show her the way out of the wilderness. Tonight, she will knock, and we will open the door for her."

She looked over to her senior team member, John, "I want you to go out to my garden and cut one of those red roses. Cut the stem long, ya hear? And I want you to put on a suit, black with a white shirt and black tie."

"Yes, Martha," he replied and walked out of the back door.

"He wants us to prepare to get His child. Lord," she openly prayed, "I'm ready to take your child. Whenever she is ready, I'll come to her. I've given her the sign, and now I'm waiting for Yours. Work through us. Amen."

Bent But Not Broken

Sara woke up to someone knocking on her door and yelling "Get the lead out girls. The van leaves in an hour. Get up, dress, and eat. Time to head to the strip!"

Pain throbbed at the stem of Sara's neck as she rolled out of her bed. It hurt to walk from all the soreness in her muscles that was so deep she felt it in her bones. She was determined to make it on her own and pushed through the pain. To move forward, she needed to push past the emptiness of grief that was growing inside of her. Having lost so much in her life, losing CC caused something inside of her to break. This cockeyed girl had helped her to cope. She showed her that within pain was hope. For the first time she had found a friend, someone who wanted nothing from her but friendship. Today Sara decided to stop being numb and uncaring as she slid a dress over her bruised skin and unpinned her hair so that it was fell gracefully down her back. She owed CC her feelings and she mourned her friend.

Sara didn't know how much longer she would be able to do this, going out night after night, hitting her mark and now, without her buddy. Stepping into the hallway she instinctively looked for her friend. The smell of her perfume, her silly giggle, or the instant headache she got when she tried to roll her eyes. Sara was met by silence and her growing anger.

SPIRITUAL WICKEDNESS IN HIGH PLACES

On the ride to the strip, Sara opened her purse and pulled out a tissue. She rubbed the raspberry lipstick she had applied earlier from her mouth. Reaching back into her purse she took out a tube of lipstick and a small compact mirror. Opening the mirror, she looked at her face. She had avoided really looking at herself. She noticed the hollow sadness in her eyes and the bite marks on her cheeks. As her eyes watered, she opened the lipstick and put it on. When the van stopped on the strip and everyone was getting out, one of the girls looked at her and said, "Damn, Trina, that red lipstick is fire, girl! The tricks are gonna love that!" Not saying a word, she stepped onto the strip and started walking the street.

Sara walked her three blocks, back and forth for several hours. She was approached repeatedly, each time she would shake her head no and walk away. Several of the men yelled at her, calling her names and threatening to kill her. A couple of them mentioned her branded shoulder and told her that they were going to call Sir. Twenty minutes before the van arrived to take them back to the ranch, a black SUV-Chevy Tahoe with tinted windows pulled up. A man got out and approached her. He leaned in, keeping his hands behind his back and whispered into her ear "Did you wear that red lipstick tonight for me?" Sara looked at him and looked at the SUV. The back window lowered, and Martha was sitting in the back, smiling at her. She nodded yes to the man and he handed her a long stem red rose in one hand while offering his other hand to her. Sara took it and walked over to the SUV. When the door opened, she got in and never looked back. The girl who had complimented her on the red lipstick noticed the van and the man who approached her. She thought as she watched the van pull away, *"Trina caught a big fish tonight; I have to get me some of that red lipstick!"*

Martha

Sara spent the next seven years with Martha. Her home was called "The Healing Heart Ministry." She grew stronger every day. For a month Martha let her have time alone. She was not asked to help; she was allowed to go out and walk through the garden. When she broke down, sometimes in the middle of a sentence, Martha would hold her and pray. She taught Sara how to balance the books and ministered to her every day. Seeing the branded S on her shoulder, Martha cried. She told Sara that she was special to God and that every night for three months, she had seen Sara's face in her dreams. God told her to go and bring his sheep home.

One night while they were drinking a cup of tea, Martha started rocking back and forth. She was praying in a strange language. Sara remembered from church that it was called speaking in tongues, except this sounded different from when Pastor or Lady Rose use to do it. With Martha it was natural, not forced. She had pushed the memories of the church from her mind but being with Martha brought it all back. After Martha stopped praying, she told Sara that God would restore her. She said that Sara had to see what was happening to those girls. That she was the sacrifice. Martha went on to say that God wanted her to spend time at Healing Hearts to prepare for her assignment.

SPIRITUAL WICKEDNESS IN HIGH PLACES

"What assignment? God has not spoken to me in years so how am I supposed to get instructions?" she asked.

Martha quietly responded "When the time is right you will know what you need to do. Just remember that obedience is better than sacrifice."

Sara listened but was skeptical. She didn't know about this church stuff anymore. Her heart had hardened, and she no longer prayed. The voice she used to know did not talk to her anymore. She agreed to stay with Martha. Not because of what Martha had told her. Truthfully, she had nowhere else to go.

In the Healing Heart Ministry, Sara found somewhere that was between a house and a home. She had grown comfortable with Martha and with the work. It had taken some time, but she was starting to exhale and just breathe. There were moments, and at first days where she felt like she was falling into an abyss. Nights were always the hardest. She often thought of CC and some of the other girls and remembered how they were all treated as if they were nothing and would wake up crying out and soaked in sweat. The demons taunted her, regret, anger, shame, fear and unworthiness.

Martha was with her in prayer. She heard every moan and groan. She felt her internal struggles and she would rise from her bed and pray. God had not given her permission to go to Sara and comfort her. It was hard to resist the urge and her calling so when Martha prayed, she called out to God for the both of them. Each morning she made her way to the kitchen to be there when Sara arrived dressed in baggy shirts and jeans, it symbolized a cocoon of protection and invisibility.

"Good morning," Martha greeted, her. "You're up again, I see. Rough night?"

Nodding, Sara took a seat at the table next to Martha. "Having your tea?"

"As always. Can I get you a mug?"

"No, it's fine." Every time Sara woke like this, she'd come out to the kitchen and sit with Martha and decline a cup of tea. Tea wouldn't help anything. Having Martha next to her is the comfort, the salve to her sensitive nerves. She glanced at Martha's Bible. "What are you reading this morning?"

"I'm reading about the story of Esther. It's amazing how many new things you read in the same chapters each time. I feel I'm being spoken to in a different way than when I last read it, even though it's only been a couple of years. God works wonderfully. Like Esther, he has great plans for you."

Sara wasn't sure about the "great plans" Martha spoke of. But she did feel she was getting stronger and more capable. Deep inside she knew that her strength was connected to Martha's prayers. Through their many conversations, Sara learned that Martha had been rescuing girls from the strip for years. Many had been taken off the street, having just disappeared. Some were seen being abducted on building security film. Others were lured through modeling scams or sold by family members. Regardless of how they ended up in a sex ring, there was never enough information to find them or their abductors. When Martha was able to help a girl, she would notify the police in their hometown. Most of the time the girls stayed with her for months before returning home.

When asked why she did this work, Martha would reply, because the Lord called me to do it. She could not tell you exactly when she started or how long she would do this work. The only thing she was certain of was that this was her purpose. Some of her team were convinced that she was an angel and as quickly as she had come, one day she would be gone. The Healing Heart ran solely on donations. Sara's job was to manage the finances and talk with donors. Sometimes she would tell part of her story. For the past year, each day Martha asked her if she was ready to go home. Each day Sara would say no. She could not go home. She was ashamed and it was better if they believed that she was dead.

During the first three years with Martha, Sara did not have the courage to search for her name on the internet. One day while Martha was away and she was preparing some requests for donations letters, she googled her name. Several stories popped up. The first, "Hope Wanes for Girl Missing for 6 years," the next story "Mother Refuses to Give Up." Sara clicked on the second story and read about her mother and family still putting up flyers for her. Candlelight vigils had dwindled from hundreds of people to just her family. Her mother was quoted as saying that she knew her daughter was alive. The abduction had broken her mother, who was now a minister. She had started her own church and worked with parents of other missing girls. The articles speculated that Sara had run off or had been abducted, either way she had vanished without a trace. The first article mentioned that there were no leads in the case and the Pastor of the young girl's church, Christopher Stanfield and his wife Rose had started a fundraiser campaign to build a new wing onto the church dedicated to Sara. Over five million dollars had been raised, yet construction had not started. *The man has no limits at all,* she thought.

The ringing phone pulled Sara attention away from the internet and back to her task at hand. Remembering her instructions, she waited for the third ring before answering. Martha told her that in case it was a donor we did not want to seem desperate. After the third ring she picked up and said "Hello, this is the Healing Heart Ministry, how can I help you."

"Hello, this is Mr. Michael Byers office. Mr. Byers has received one of your solicitation letters and is considering donating to your organization. He would like to come and tour your facilities and meet your executive director while he is in the area. Is that possible?" she said.

"Yes, it is. Martha is not here at the moment, but I can check her calendar to see if she is available." After a few moments of silence , "Sara continued, "It looks like she can meet with him tomorrow afternoon. If he can come for lunch, that would be perfect."

"Lunch will work with his schedule. Mr. Byers does not like pizza or fried foods. He is allergic to nuts and does not drink alcohol. If you can accommodate his dietary constraints that would be appreciated. If not, we can arrange for food to be delivered," the lady said.

Sara chuckled and replied "I am sure that we can manage. We look forward to hosting Mr. Byers tomorrow."

When Martha returned home, Sara told her that some man named Byers called and wanted to visit because he is thinking about donating. She told Martha that the man must be delicate because there is a list of stuff he can't eat.

"What's his name again?" Martha asked.

"Mr. Byers." Sara replied.

"As in Michael Byers?"

"Yep, that is the one."

"Sara, Michael Byers is not delicate, he is wealthy. That man is the head of Byers Technology. He is worth billions! Did they say why he is interested in The Healing Heart?" Martha asked.

"Nope" Sara replied.

She did not care about rich men. Her experience had taught her that rich men were mean, nasty, hateful, and brutal. She wanted nothing to do with the man and would make sure that she stayed out of sight.

SPIRITUAL WICKEDNESS IN HIGH PLACES

The next day Martha spent the morning walking through the house making sure that everything was tidy. She had picked vegetables from her garden and prepared grilled salmon and a fresh garden salad. The night before she baked a pecan pie. Sara was amazed at how well-rested Martha looked. She heard her rambling around in the kitchen until after midnight. Each time she entered and offered to help; Martha shooed her out. Mr. Byers was scheduled to arrive at noon. She decided to hang around until 11:30 then duck out of sight.

The doorbell rang at 11:00. Martha pulled off her apron and went to answer the door. It was Michael Byers. *"Ugh,"* Sara thought. She would have to walk past this guy to get to her room. Michael reached for Martha's hand and thanked her for agreeing to meet with him on such short notice. She led him to the back of the house where her office was located. Passing Sara in the hallway, Martha stopped and introduced her to Michael. He was an older man with grey hair. He was slender and about two inches taller than Sara. He stuck out his hand and Sara shook it. Then clasping her hand in both of his. She pulled away, intimidated by his innocent aggression of clasping her hand. He apologized for being so forward and told her that he was happy to meet her. Martha took him by the arm and led him into her office. Sara went to her room and did not give him a second thought.

During their meeting Martha learned that Michael's granddaughter had been lured into meeting a man through a dating app. She was missing for five years before they found her body floating in Quinn River just northwest of Las Vegas, in Humboldt county. She had been wrapped in a sheet and had a rope with pieces of plastic wrapped around her neck. Her name was Elizabeth.

Michael told Martha that he felt like he had to do something and decided that he would research and visit programs that were helping girls who were being sex trafficked. He became aware of the Healing Heart through a solicitation letter that was handed to him by his pastor.

Martha gave him a tour of her home and explained to him how God leads her to the girls as they become ready. She said that there were other people who helped her pick them up since this was the most dangerous part of what they do. Immediately drawn to her and impressed by what he had seen and heard, Michael asked, how he could help.

"Well," Martha replied, "I would get a bigger house. Right now, I only take a few girls at a time. I would like to help more but I can only help when I have the resources. I would also start a job training program. I would like to hire staff that can help with counseling and drug addiction. You know some of my girls are ready to go home right away. But some, like in Sara's case, it has been over three years and she is not ready to even let people know that she is alive and well."

"Martha, can you share her story with me?" he asked.

Martha and Michael had lunch on the deck near the flower garden. While they ate, Martha shared Sara's story. Several times she noticed Michael wiping his eyes with his handkerchief. He listened without interrupting. He stopped eating halfway through the story and glanced up towards the sky. Gently shaking his head. He asked how men could be so evil. Martha looked at him and sat back in her chair.

She said, "For some, it is about power over others. They lack control of their own fate and circumstances, so they take it out on anyone that is weak. These women are taken. They are broken and beaten by animals. Many suffer in their own homes in silence. You know," she continued, "God revealed something to me a long time ago. Through his word he showed me the strength and power of women. So much so that he asks us and only us, to submit ourselves under a Godly husband. Not because we are less than, but because we are equal to and in some ways greater than. We represent the heart of God. As for Sara, her journey is about something different. She is not

SPIRITUAL WICKEDNESS IN HIGH PLACES

a victim. God is preparing her to break down and destroy those who are the shepherds of spiritual wickedness in high places. They are the most dangerous men of all."

Michael had many more questions but decided to wait and ask them later. He had a feeling that he and Martha would be lifelong friends and work together to do great things. "Martha," he said, "I want to start a foundation dedicated to helping and healing young women. I will call it Beth's Healing Heart Foundation, and I want your organization to be our first grantee. We will start with a three-million-dollar grant, what do you think?" He waited. "Martha?"

"Wait a minute," she said, "I need to be able to minister God's word in my own way to these girls. I need to select my own people, and…and I need something else, but I can't think of it right now. Can you promise me that?"

Michael laughing replied, "My friend, you will co-chair the board with me. So, these are all your shots to call!"

Martha let out a scream, jumped out of her chair praising God and dancing in circles. Michael asked her what was in her tea and she replied, "Holy Water!"

As she settled into her chair, fanning her face, Michael said he had one request.

"Oh, here we go," said Martha, "There is always something, isn't there?"

"I want to help Sara. Do you think it would help her if I gave her a job?" he asked.

Martha, looking towards the house, closed her eyes. She held up her hand to signal she needed a minute to think. She prayed, "*Lord, you know that I am protective of this child, but you have work for her to do. What should I do, please give me the words, and let me hold on to the favor that you have given me with this man? In Jesus' name I pray. Amen.*" Slowly Martha opened her eyes. She looked at Michael and said, "Sara can work for you, but she must remain here until she is ready to do more."

"Deal," he responded and reached across the table to seal the partnership with a handshake. Martha slapped his hand away and asked for a holy hug.

Later that evening, Martha told Sara about Michael's offer. She loved the idea of making her own money and not having to leave the safety of the Healing Heart made the idea even better. As the years passed, she grew more and more confident. Michael placed her over donor relations and eventually she began traveling by private jet to meet with him and prospective donors. She shared stories of the girls and talked about what their futures could look like. Michael was more than pleased with Sara. He would look at her and imagine that if Beth were alive, she would be just like her. One thing was sure, when Sara spoke with donors, the size of their gifts increased. She had come a long way. Confident and strong. She had become fearless.

The Return

Sara loved her work but lately, she thought more and more about going home. It was a nagging urge that she could not shake. She decided that it was time to tell Martha that she was ready. What she could not share with Martha was why she felt the need to go home. She was going to kill Pastor. She had to make an example of him and stop him. She knew that it would hurt Martha and the foundation. Deep down inside she hoped that it would help the foundation, so she wrote a letter explaining how to spin the murder to further support the need to help women like her. She placed the letter into an envelope and gave it to one of the girls in the house, instructing her to not give it to Martha for four weeks. Later that evening she told Martha that she would be flying home in two days.

"It is time for me to go home, Martha," she said.

"Will you be back?"

"I don't know. I hope so."

"Did the Lord speak?"

"I don't think so, but I know there are some things I need to do."

"I will be praying for you, Sara"

"I've no doubt that you will."

The night before her departure Sara had trouble sleeping. What she needed to do would hurt a lot of people. Her mother would be devastated to have her daughter return to lose her to prison and possibly lethal injection. Her siblings will have to deal with the media, but they will be all right. They had all grown and moved on with their lives. In her mind she felt more than justified with the planned course of action. She assumed that Chris Stanfield used the alias of JJ. So, killing him would end the abduction of young girls in Elkhart.

For months, she had secretly left Martha's house three days each week and went to the gun range. She took classes and found out that although she was right-handed, she was spot on shooting with her left. Flirting with her instructor she was able to manipulate him into giving her a gun. He gave her a Glock 17, Gen 4 semi-automatic pistol. It was the full-size model. He included two full clips and a leather carrying bag. She had lied to Martha about where she was going and what she was doing. When asked, she told her that she was getting things ready for her trip home.

Thinking through her next steps, Sara decided that it would be better to plan how she would kill Pastor Stanfield once she arrived in Elkhart and got settled. This way, she could establish her bearings. She hoped to get lucky and catch him and Calvin together, allowing her to get even and stop both of them. She would move back to Elkhart and bide her time until an opportunity presented itself. She knew the entire town would turn against her for killing a beloved pastor. However, this fact was not a deterrent. He had taken something precious from her and for that, he would not receive any mercy nor forgiveness. The time has come.

The morning of her flight, she got up early and walked into the kitchen. Martha was sitting at the table enjoying a cup of coffee, bacon and eggs and a short stack of silver dollar pancakes.

"Oh, my goodness. The food smells amazing and I am starving."

"There is more over there," Martha said while pointing toward the stove.

SPIRITUAL WICKEDNESS IN HIGH PLACES

"I want everything but the bacon. You know I don't fool with the pig," Sara said reflecting on Sir's slimy smelly pork breath.

Sara sat her plate on the table and walked to the counter to pour a cup of coffee. Martha looked at her plate and took note that she had very little food on it. "I thought you were starving," she said.

"I'm nervous about heading home. My stomach says it's hungry, but my appetite disagrees."

Martha replied, "I know going home is tough. Just remember to take one day at a time with your Mom. Ease back into things. I will call you in a couple of weeks. Remember to check your email. I will send work related stuff through there. Most of all, I need you to pray. Let God lead you and everything will work out."

Sara half listened to Martha's advice. She was not going to pray, and she knew that everything was going to work out because she was going to see to it.

Intuition

Minister Jennifer Robinson had dedicated the last nineteen years of her life to caring for the families with missing girls. Since her daughter disappeared, she could not spend a moment being idle. After reuniting with her husband, she quit her job and searched for Sara. She put flyers up everywhere and asked everyone she met if they had seen her daughter or heard anything. For the first year, Jason Johnson would pick her up and drive her around between his taxi runs. She would talk to him about Sara. After several months without any leads, he encouraged her to move on. He said that he knew that is what Sara would want her to do. That statement frustrated Jen because she knew it was not true. Her daughter would want her family to keep looking. As the years went on, the fight to keep Sara alive in her mind grew harder to win.

Prior to Sara vanishing, one other young girl had gone missing. No one thought much about it because she had a reputation of being loose. Since Sara, a girl went missing every eighteen months, vanishing without a trace. Some were from Elkhart and others from Mishawaka and South Bend. All of the towns were only twenty minutes away. As far as Jen was concerned, the cops were worthless, so she organized to help do what the police department seemed to be unable to do.

SPIRITUAL WICKEDNESS IN HIGH PLACES

It was a Saturday night; Jen was hosting another dinner for her families. She stopped by Wilts Grocery store to pick up a few items, including one of Betty Wilts' pies. The Wilts had been truly kind to her. They used to stop by with food and once a week they would deliver groceries. Betty would always give her a hug and Jen felt like there was something she wanted to say but would not or could not do it. Betty had decided that she would never tell anyone about the pregnancy test. She did not want people to think that she had pushed Sara to hurt herself or run away.

Standing in the aisle looking for paper plates, Jen overheard Betty and Rose, Pastor Stanfield's wife, talking about a strange woman who had shown up in church Sunday. Rose mentioned that no one seemed to know her, and the woman had left before service ended. They gossiped about how strange it was and wonder whose husband the woman might be having an affair. Betty asked Rose if she noticed that the woman sat in Sara's old seat. Rose said that the woman ought to be careful, she might come up missing next.

Jen stepped around the corner, catching the women off guard. "Praise the Lord church," she said.

Betty and Rose looked as if they had seen a ghost. Hanging their heads, they responded in unison, "Praise the Lord."

Rose reached for Jen's hand and started apologizing for being so insensitive. She was not sure what had come over her. Jen ignored the gesture and told them all was forgiven. "It has been trying times for everyone," she said.

Rose felt bad. She didn't like who she had become. Sara had been close to her and she missed her. Whenever she tried to talk to Chris about Sara, he would become angry and admonish her for gossiping. She demanded more of herself and vowed to stop by Jen's house to see how she could help with her ministry.

While standing in line to check out, Jen started thinking about what the two women were discussing and wondered if it could possibly be Sara. She shrugged off the thought, knowing that if it were Sara, she would have come home to her first.

Several days later, Jen was driving through the old factory district on her way to the northside of town to pick up a mom whose daughter had been missing for over a year. She noticed a woman with a long ponytail jogging. She thought the woman resembled Sara. The jogger darted between two of the old factory buildings. Jen turned the car around and circled the block thinking the woman would have to emerge on the street somewhere behind the buildings. By the time she got there, the woman was nowhere in sight.

Over the next several days, Jen drove through the district, hoping to catch another glance of the woman but she never showed up again. Second guessing her intuition and what she had seen, Jen told her husband about the sighting and he warned her not to get worked up about it. He reminded her that Sara loved her family too much to not come home if she could. She agreed but deep in the center of her being she knew that woman was her daughter and wondered why she had not come home and more importantly, why was she hiding. Could it be that she felt that she was in danger?

Recalling the conversation, she heard earlier between Rose and Betty, Jen decided to watch the church to see if the woman showed up again. Maybe the strange woman who showed up for that Sunday service would show up again. She parked across the street on Sundays and Wednesdays for two weeks and watched the people as they entered and left. Without any sighting of the strange woman, she made up her mind that she would watch through Sunday night revival service and, if the woman did not show up, she would follow her husband's advice and let it go.

JJ

JJ drove his car into the gated parking garage of his penthouse apartment in South Bend. He never used the valet service. The less contact he had with people close to his home the better. Each day he would leave and return to his apartment using the service elevator. His privacy was important to him. A man in his line of business should not draw a lot of attention.

At forty-five, he had done well for himself. He did not keep close ties with anyone. Most people would be surprised to know that he maintained a penthouse. He had kept his parent's home in Elkhart and would spend at least two nights a week there. His neighbors thought his absence was due to his work schedule.

The house he grew up in was never a home. It was a place of meanness and manipulation. Watching his father beat his mom and make her serve both of them, he quickly learned that a man's role was to rule over a woman. His mother was resentful and ungrateful. She was pitiful. JJ remembered one night when his father had beaten his mother. As she laid on the floor bleeding, his father told her to go into the bedroom and undress. She quickly, without fighting back, went into the bedroom and closed the door. His father walked into the kitchen and poured a shot of whiskey. After downing the drink in one gulp, he walked past JJ and winked. He then walked into the bedroom and, leaving the door open, had sex with his mother while his son watched. His mother enjoyed it. She responded to his father's touch, moaning, and begging for more and when finished, they would lay in bed together laughing and talking. He was ten years old. From that day forward his father demanded the door remain open.

After graduating high-school, JJ went to college. During his freshman year he met so many girls willing to have sex with him. Making good grades came easy and he quickly earned the reputation of being smart. In high school, he would help girls cheat if they had sex with him. In college, he was able to convince girls to sleep with his friends in exchange for help with their papers. What they did not know is that he would make his friends pay him.

Over the years, JJ built a strong sex trafficking business. Through his fraternity, he made connections with organized crime and quickly learned the business and earned respect. His business model was solid. He would attend churches and identify preachers who were spreading a prosperity message or those who passed the offering plate several times throughout the service. He knew that these men were desperate and loved money, flash, and importance.

After each service he would linger behind and introduce himself as a businessman looking for a church home he could support. The response was universal. They eagerly took him in. In each town, JJ would set up a men's club called "The Brotherhood." He let the pastors recruit others. Initially, he would present them with alcohol and good food. After a few months, he would provide women. For some, the younger the better. Next, he engaged them in identifying women who they could mark as "belonging to them" and were easy prey for abduction. The criteria, they had to be attractive, come from a broken or troubled home, or enjoyed male attention. In exchange, he made large donations to their churches and gave each man ten percent of the money made off of each woman until she was no longer profitable.

The men in the church quickly took to the program. They formed quickly, kept secrets, and started to supply targets. JJ had six "Brotherhoods" across northern Indiana and southern Michigan. He would rotate visiting them, often working the bar and serving them drinks. This allowed him to observe them and tape them while they indulged their fantasies. Taping them was a security measure he could use in the event someone suddenly developed a conscience. It kept them quiet and in the game. Business was going well, and he wanted to keep it that way.

Unfortunately, a problem had arrived in Elkhart. He was the first to identify that one of the girls had returned to the city. He had called Chris and told him that they needed to meet. The church was having a revival which ended on the coming Sunday. He would meet with Chris after church to discuss how they would handle it.

Revival

Sara had tacked the bulletin she had picked up from the church on her refrigerator. It announced the "Restoration Revival" and invited people to attend church each night. It promised attendees that each night they would be delivered from an attack on their marriages, relationships, finances, and jobs. Sunday would be the last night to hear the message, *take a step of faith by tithing and receive restoration.*

"So, Sunday is the day," Sara thought, "I have three days to prepare." She remembered the revivals when she attended the church. On the last night, the Pastor and Associate Pastor Calvin Peterson would stay after service to count the final tithes and prepare the bank deposit. Everyone else would head home exhausted. Even the church missionaries and youth groups would wait until Monday to come back to the church and clean up.

Feeling antsy, Sara decided to go to the gun range and practice. It would help her work off the nervous energy and think. Her concern was not accuracy but controlling her nerves. One of the safety monitors at the range noticed her hand shaking. He told her to breathe through it and if it helped to image someone she didn't like. She thought, *"If you only knew."* Leaving the gun range she decided to return to her apartment and go for a run before turning in for the night.

SPIRITUAL WICKEDNESS IN HIGH PLACES

Three days passed quickly. Sara felt that she was ready for the most important day of her life. She waited until 11:00 pm. She figured that the revival would end at 10:00. She gave 30 minutes for the people to talk and clear out and another fifteen mins for the missionaries to end their parking lot meetings and go home. She decided that she would jog to the church. At 10:45, dressed in a black athletic leotard running suit, black running shoes, and a black scarf tied around her head. She pulled on a shoulder holster and stuffed the Glock inside. She eased into the alley behind her building, checked to see that no one was watching and headed for the church.

The revival had been a huge success. From the looks of the offering basket, the money had poured in. The baskets were circulated three times and each round all of them returned full to the brim. Pastor Stanfield felt that the church was in a good place. Each night the attendance at the revival had grown and tonight there was standing room only.

Sensing the weariness of the members, he cut his sermon short by thirty minutes. After the people had cleared out Rose decided to use the extra time to clean up a little. She asked a couple of the missionaries to stay over and help her. Pastor Stanfield had nodded in approval and asked Calvin to join him and JJ in the office to talk and prepare the nightly deposit. He had noticed JJ entering the church halfway through his sermon and taking his seat on the first pew.

Rose had noticed JJ enter as well. Anytime he showed up, she knew that Chris was going to be out late. This men's group was a mystery to her. Lately, her husband had treated her harsher than normal. He had a way of making her feel stupid and worthless. Ironically, in front of the congregation he went on and on about how beautiful and virtuous she was. He never mentioned that he had not been intimate with his beautiful wife for months at a time and when he was, he was selfish.

Pastor Stanfield, Calvin and JJ entered his office. Calvin walked over to a small table in the corner of the office and started counting the money from the night's offerings. Pastor Stanfield walked over to a cabinet behind his desk and pulled out a bottle of scotch. He set three glasses on his desk and poured into each one. He called out to Calvin, holding a glass out in one hand while handing JJ a glass with the other hand. He lifted his glass and offered a toast. JJ interrupted him, "We have a more serious matter to discuss before we start celebrating," he said.

Chris lowered his glass and asked what could be so important.

"Sara is back," he stated.

"What! Are you sure?" Chris asked.

"Hell, yeah, I'm sure. I picked her up and brought her to your church a few weeks ago."

"The mystery woman. Damn JJ, why are you just telling me this!"

"And exactly what were you going to do about it? I've been watching her. She went to the gun range Wednesday. Now that may mean nothing, then again it may mean something," JJ said.

Calvin gulped his drink and coughed as he paced back and forth. He knew that this was not good at all. *If the woman was keeping her return quiet, she was up to no good*, he thought. "Listen, JJ, we need to take her out. That bitch will bring the house down around us if she starts talking. I can't go to jail man," he said.

"Calm down Calvin, that is precisely why I am here," JJ replied.

SPIRITUAL WICKEDNESS IN HIGH PLACES

Jen sat patiently in her car watching the church. She saw the lot empty quickly and only five cars remained. She knew who owned three of the cars: Pastor Stanfield, Lady Rose and Calvin Roberson, the Associate Pastor. She thought the other car belonged to Jason Johnson and wondered who had called an Uber. As she was about to call it a night and leave, she saw something move at the back of the lot. Holding her breath, she watched what looked like a woman, dressed in black moving towards the back door of the church. Not sure who it was or what she should do, she continued to watch as the woman enter the church.

Entering the church, Sara stood in the doorway. A set of steps to the left led downstairs to the basement, where the kitchen and dining areas were located. The steps directly in front of her lead to the back hallway where the Sunday school classrooms were and the Pastor's office. Sara could hear women's voices coming from below. The only lights in the hallway were the emergency exit sign and a light underneath the door to the Pastor's office.

She quietly eased up the stairs, careful to walk on the edge to avoid any risk of squeaky steps. She eased down the hallway. She could hear men talking. Three distinct voices. She heard her name and clearly heard Calvin yell, "Kill her." Sara pulled the gun out of her holster and opened the door. The men hesitated for a few seconds before realizing their situation, their eyes scouring the room for any bid at escape. Calvin walked towards her, and she fired a shot to the right of his head, grazing the top of his ear.

She motioned for him to join Chris and JJ. As Calvin complied, she focused on JJ. "Jason Johnson, you sick fuck," she said.

"Sara wait," Chris said, "you don't know what you are doing. Put the gun down and let's talk about everything."

Sara fired off another round, hitting Chris in the arm. Tears started flowing down her cheeks, but she refused to blink.

"Wait, Sara, wait!" JJ yelled, almost shrieking. "Is it— Is it money you want, Sara? I can get you money. I can more than make up for what happened. Really, Sara, I can. I just need you to put the gun down and tell me the number. I'll get it right away, Sara, really. What do you want two million, three? Just name your price. You don't want to do this," he said.

"Sara, you will not get out of this room alive if you try to do this. Tell us what the hell you want, and let's end this now before someone gets hurt," Chris said.

Rose heard the first shot and told the ladies to call the police. She rushed up the back stairs and heard a second shot coming from the Pastor's office. As she approached the doorway, she heard a woman's voice and stopped, leaned against the wall and listened.

Sara quickly wiped her tears on her shoulder and noticed the rose tattoo. She looked at Chris and, rocking side to side, maintained a steady aim moving from one man to the other. Through tears she said, "You raped me! You gave me to people who cut my baby— our baby from my stomach. You sold me like a piece of trash to men who abused my body. You took everything from me. And if that was not bad enough, you took God from me. You destroyed my faith, my hope, my joy. You all stand in high places and prey on the innocent. You are soulless and need to return to the hell hole you crawled out of," she said. "Why—" The tears cut Sara off from finishing, she swallowed the lump rising in her throat and pushed through. "Why shouldn't I kill you?"

SPIRITUAL WICKEDNESS IN HIGH PLACES

"Because daughter, if you kill them, there is no coming back from that," Rose said as she placed her hand on her shoulder. "Give me the gun and leave this ungodly place."

Sara started to resist, but Rose squeezed her shoulder again. She leaned over and whispered into Sara's ear "Obedience is better than Sacrifice." Sara relaxed her shoulders and shakily transferred the gun into Rose's hands.

"Now go," Rose said.

Sara backed out of the office and stumbled against the wall. For a moment she stood, bracing herself, her mind racing. This was not the plan. Her entire reason for being here was to stop these evil people. She took a step towards the door, when Lady Rose called out to her again, "Get out of here daughter!".

There was an authority within her voice and for a second, Sara thought she sounded exactly like Martha. Regardless, this was a command and instinctually she turned and swiftly walked to the front of the church, passing by the darkened offices and ignoring the chattering and yelling behind her. She glanced up at the crucifix behind the pulpit, lowered her head and walked out the front doors. Stumbling down the steps, she grabbed the railing with her sweaty palms. Doubling over, she wailed, releasing a piercing and deep sound that cut through all of the darkness around her. Between each scream a gunshot rang out. There were three of them. Upon hearing the third shot, Sara fell to her knees in a ball. She crossed her arms in front of her grabbing each shoulder and began gently rocking back and forth.

After hearing the gunshots, a few minutes later Jen saw the woman dressed in black bursting through the door and stumbling down the stairs. She got out of her car and ran as fast as she could to the woman, the hunched figure breaking her heart as she let out a wrenching cry.

As she reached the steps she said, "Sara."

Sara looked up into the face of an angel. Her mother grabbed her and held her, both rocking back and forth and crying. She clenched her mother for dear life, allowing the loving arms to envelope her.

Rose pointed the gun at the three men. Unlike Sara's, her vision was unblurred, clear and focused and determined. She was done with all of this, with the wickedness and the cover ups and always being told it was her fault, that she just wasn't *woman* enough for everything. No, Chris just wasn't *man* enough. She let out a breath.

"Rose, put that gun down before you regret it."

She said nothing, just stared at him.

"Stupid woman put the gun down! You're not doing anything. If I have to take it from you…"

"Get your wife in order man!" JJ demanded, looking to Chris.

Slowly, Calvin eased from behind the desk.

In a clean shot, Rose nailed Chris in the head, hitting him right between the eyes.

Calvin dropped to the floor, praying and crying.

JJ ducked at first. But the moment he lifted his head, Rose shot him, taking off the top of his skull.

Calvin's groans deepened once he heard the second shot. "Rose—Sister Rose, please. You don't want to do this, please. You don't want to. You can let me go. It's not too late. Oh, God. Dear God, save my soul, Lord, please. Rose, you don't have to…" He devolved into more tearful babbling.

"You better keep praying," Rose said as she walked closer to him.

SPIRITUAL WICKEDNESS IN HIGH PLACES

As he lowered his head, she shot him in the back of it.

Gun in hand, Rose walked out of the office, her heels echoing in the silent halls.

Four police cars drove up, and as they got out of their cars, three gunshots rang out. They noticed a young woman doubled over and screaming between each shot. Another woman was running towards her. As they embraced, each turned their attention to the police who hid behind their cars, guns drawn. The police continued to signal each other. Someone yelled " Sarge" and pointed to the church. An officer yelled, "Drop it, I said drop the gun! Listen to me Lady Rose, I am not going to tell you again. Please drop the gun and raise your hands!"

Jen and Sara saw Rose standing at the top of the steps, gun in hand. She raised both arms in the air, fingers spread wide, letting the gun fall to the ground. She looked at Sara and smiled. The police ran to her and pulled her arms behind her. After placing handcuffs on her wrist, they led her to the squad cars. Passing Jen on the steps, Rose mouthed, "I'm sorry."

Jen watched as the police placed Rose into the back of the squad car. Sara laid her head on her mother's shoulder and heard the voice that she had lost twenty years ago say, *"Well done my good and faithful servant. Welcome Home."*

Epilogue

"I'm happy to announce that, by God's grace and hard work, the new Esther's House shelter for women and girls victimized by sex trafficking is open!"

Light spilled into the sanctuary of the church as Pastor Stanfield's replacement, Pastor Deborah Matthias, stood in front of the altar with a beaming smile. She waited for the applause to die down and cleared her throat. "You're clapping but you don't see the two women who made this all possible. Sara, Jen, come up here, please."

Sara had returned to the seats she and her siblings once occupied years ago. Only this time she's returned with her whole family and the peace she hadn't felt in years.

This shelter had been her and her mother's brainchild. Starting with the girl's recovered from the Brotherhood, she planned to help others like her, the same way Martha had shown her. She had become God's messenger of abounding grace and unfailing love.

"Oh, don't be shy," Pastor Matthias said, opening her arms and waving them up.

Taking her mother's hand, Sara came to her feet and walked down the long aisle to the podium, her chest swelling with both excitement and nervousness. Even now, attention made her uncomfortable. After years of the wrong sort, she felt she had the right to feel some anxiety. Nonetheless, she smiled at the adoring faces.

Blinking away the tears, her mind was only on one thing, that voice. She thought of Martha who seemly had vanished, leaving The Healing Hearts ministry in the hands of her faithful team. She was last seen walking in the desert. John, her faithful driver, had dropped her off and watched her walk away. He had only looked away for a second, but when he returned his gaze to the sport where he last saw her, she was nowhere in sight. Now with Mr. Byers and her family with her she vowed to speak life into the hearts of others, to live in each moment of each day and to never forget that greater is he that is within her than anything that is within the world.

"Never take your own revenge, beloved, but leave room for the wrath of God, for it is written, "VENGEANCE IS MINE, I WILL REPAY," saith the Lord." - *Romans* 12:19

www.ingramcontent.com/pod-product-compliance
Lightning Source LLC
LaVergne TN
LVHW090056080526
838200LV00097B/392/J